For Phoebe, my beautiful niece, a light
bearer in the world.

ISBN 9781698487090

CONTENTS

PART ONE
THE BEGINNING

Chapter One
Abnormally Perfect

Mr and Mrs Wortol were perfectly normal, or maybe abnormally perfect...or so it seemed to their neighbours, who scrutinised their every move looking to point out their faults. But, the biggest fault they could find was that they didn't seem to have any and that made the neighbours nervous. "A lack of flaws on the surface meant there must be deep secrets buried beneath," rumoured the neighbours.

Mrs Wortol was a stay-at-home mother or housewife, whichever people prefer. She was a petit woman with red hair. Her eyes were kind and like a still green sea.

Mr Wortol had an athletic build, which confused the

neighbours; they never saw him do any exercise and his job certainly didn't call for strenuous labour. Mr Wortol left home every morning in a suit, with a briefcase in hand and climbed into his little car peering through rectangular spectacles. He clearly had an office job, not that the neighbours knew what it was. He had a perfect side parting in his chestnut brown hair. When he kissed his wife and children, William and Jessica, he tickled their faces with his neatly trimmed moustache and beard. They were a beautiful family. The perfect family. No-one would have realised there was anything unusual about them, no matter how much they wanted there to be.

Mr and Mrs Wortol did everything they could to keep their secret under wraps. They had already moved house once because of a slip-up. No lasting damage done, just safer to move before William, being only six at the time, let the cat out of the bag, so to speak. They had been in their current house for three years now and managed to keep on top of William so far, but their new daughter was proving to be more difficult. She was spirited at only a few months old.

The Wortols were very fortunate that it was winter and Mrs Wortol could keep the pram covered for the next few months and keep their daughter from revealing their secret.

This was exactly the situation on the day this family's life would be changed forever and not for the first time for Mrs Wortol. Jessica was lying in her pram under a waterproof cover as light snow floated down onto it. William held onto the pram with his small hand whilst Mrs Wortol pushed it along and Mr Wortol adjusted his hat and scarf to keep more of the snow off. They headed out to the park for an early winter walk in the first snow. They wandered along the road edged with trees. A black crow landed on a branch above them and dusted them all lightly in more snow.

The Wortols continued to journey to the park, the sun shone extra bright in the snow filled white sky. The crow cawed behind them now. Another landed above them unnoticed on the street lamp they were passing. Silently, this continued to happen at every tree and street lamp they went by. If the Wortols had noticed, they may have thought twice about continuing their walk to the park.

Mr Wortol walked in silence with a broad smile on his face watching William tilt his face to the sky and catch snowflakes on his green-mittened hand. William giggled as his mitten turned from green to white. He didn't talk yet, even at six, but his actions spoke clearly. Every few minutes Mr Wortol would sweep his brown-gloved hand across the pram cover to prevent it from bowing under the weight of the quickly collecting snow.

As they reached the gates of the park, which were already open wide and inviting, William shook his hand free of snow so much that his mitten dropped to the ground. It was a few minutes or so later that Mr Wortol realised and backtracked to the gate. It was then that he noticed all the birds in each tree along the road and atop the street lamps. He thought he could see bats too. They went so far back that some only looked like black dots.

Mr Wortol didn't like the look of it at all. He turned back to his family who were halfway between the gate where he stood, and the lake, which was white with a layer of ice. He looked up at the trees that lined the park. More birds... more than normal. Not just a few per tree. He turned back and peered down his road. The birds and maybe bats had flocked together and were flying in his direction. They flew overhead cawing madly. Those in the trees above him joined in the chorus of caws.

The flock moved swiftly like a black plane as they moved as one in the sky. They began to drop lower as they approached his family. Suddenly, they dive-bombed the pram. Mrs Wortol let out a scream. The creatures in the trees flapped their wings wildly and took flight in the same direction. Mr Wortol raced towards the pram and began to kick and punch the winged creatures with all his might. Nobody noticed as William let go of the pram and ran away in fear. He ran as fast as his little legs could carry him. He was by the edge of the iced lake before Mr Wortol looked up and spotted him. That's not all he spotted; the flock of beasts from the park trees hadn't joined the attack of the pram, they were heading after William.

William briefly looked back at his family, but seeing the birds firing themselves in his direction, he ran onto the lake. Mr Wortol raced across the snowy grass. He reached the edge just as the ice gave way beneath William as a solitary crow dived at William and battered him through the ice.

Mr Wortol was still running as he watched willing William to resurface. The ice on the lake broke much easier under the weight of Mr Wortol and he had to wade through the icy water before he could swim. His clothes stuck to him and made him heavier and it was hard for him to swim.

Still, William and the crow hadn't resurfaced. Mr Wortol disappeared under the dark lake. Mrs Wortol was at the edge of the lake with a trail of winged beasts after her and the pram, screaming for help from any neighbour nearby.

Suddenly, as Mrs Wortol looked out over the lake she saw a small body rise out of the water and a hand push it onto the edge of the ice and then the hand was snatched back into the dark depths.

Within what felt like hours but was in fact minutes, the bats and birds had gone and Mrs Wortol, Jessica in her pram and William were instead surrounded by the emergency services. All eyes watched the lake, but Mr Wortol never surfaced.

Nearly seven years later, and they no longer looked like the perfect family. An aura of sadness surrounded them... the three of them: Mrs Wortol, Jessica and Billy, a nickname William grew to prefer to his real name. They no longer lived in a neighbourhood that watched them and marvelled at them and pondered their abnormal perfection. Now they seemed perfectly normal, like everyone else. So normal no one paid them any attention in their tiny ground floor flat. The morning shadow crept over the overgrown garden lawn and made the living room appear dimmer than it already was, even in sunshine.

The mantelpiece held photographs of the children over the last few years. There wasn't a single photo of either Mrs or Mr Wortol. On the left were photographs of Billy and Jessica when they were babies; in the middle, as they got older; and ending on the right hand side with the most recent photograph that included them both. Their first school photograph together taken towards the end of Jessica's first school year and Billy's last Primary school year.

A sudden blast of music rumbled through the flat from the apartment above them. "You may as well get up for school now!" called Mrs Wortol to Billy. She knew full well he would awake to the music even if Jessica didn't. Jessica seemed to be able to sleep through anything.

Billy sat up and yawned, adjusting to the bright light streaming through his and Jessica's bedroom window. They had no curtains, just some nets to give a little privacy.

He kicked his covers off and threw his legs over the side of the bed and onto the threadbare carpet. He peered over at his younger sister sound asleep despite the vibrations of the booming music.

"How do you sleep through it all?" he asked her, not expecting an answer.

He didn't mind being woken up. He had once again been dreaming about the crows and the lake. He was being sucked into the darkness and his lungs were filling with ice-cold black water. He hated reliving the nightmare again and again. It was better than the alternative dream where he did awful things for a creature he called 'Master'. His nightmares seemed to flick between the two.

"Billy, when you're up I'll make a move!" Mrs Wortol called to him.

"I'm just coming out of my room now!" he called back as he closed the bedroom door behind him, leaving his sister in dreamland.

Billy stretched his arms to the ceiling and shuffled sleepily towards the kitchen.

"Morning. Right, I'm going to work," she said as she bent forward and kissed him on the top of his mop of golden curls, an act she didn't perform a lot nowadays, "but at least I've seen you this morning." She smiled meekly at him and backed out towards the front door. "Bye!" she called before slamming the door behind her, which was the only way to close it because of the dodgy lock.

"Bye, Mum!" he called after her through the wooden door. She probably never heard him.

Jessica appeared in the kitchen yawning and rubbing the sleep from her eyes. Her red pigtails askew on the sides of her head and her pink pony pyjamas hanging loosely on her small frame. They were still too big for her. "The door slamming woke me up," she said.

Billy smirked. "The music can blare all night and all morning and you're snoring, but Mum closes the door and you're awake," he said finding it amusing.

"Has Mum gone to work, again?" asked Jessica.

"You know she has, Jess," he replied.

Jessica looked at him sadly. However much Jessica loved her big brother, he could never be her mother. But, he was an excellent big brother. That thought turned her frown upside down. She pulled a wooden chair away from the table of the little dining set that sat against the wall in the kitchen. The table was less than a metre square. One chair stuck out into the small space in the kitchen, another blocked the doorway when in use, which is where Jessica had planted herself and the other chair was wedged between the sink and the table, which is where she normally sat when all three of them were home...which was rare.

"What do you want for breakfast?" Billy asked.

"Chocolate flakes."

"We still don't have them," said Billy.

Jessica sighed. "Why?"

"Mum hasn't got enough money."

"But she's working all the time, why doesn't she have enough?"

"She has to make sure we have the roof over our head and food and water. Chocolate flavoured things are a luxury, we don't need them," he tried to explain.

"I *need* them," she whined.

"No, Jess, you want them; you don't need them." It was futile trying to explain the difference between 'want' and 'need' to a tired and hungry five year old.

"What do we have?"

"Cornflakes or rice pops."

"Rice pops, then," she said huffing and leaning on her elbow on the table.

Billy made them both the same, but gave half his share of milk to Jessica, so that she at least would have nearly a covering.

After breakfast Billy got his sister ready for school and then prepared himself. He appeared just in time to leave for school. His knobbly knees stuck out below a poorly stitched pair of shorts.

"When did you get shorts?" asked Jessica.

"I didn't. I cut up the trousers as I don't need them after this year and they were swinging round my ankles anyway!" Billy hated going to school in his dishevelled clothes that were too small for him. The other children laughed at him cruelly. "Come on, let's get going!" He grabbed the lunches their mother had made and gently pushed Jessica out the door and slammed it behind them. They walked to school passing a single crow. *Nothing to worry about,* thought Billy thinking about his dream, *it's just one.*

They reached the school gates and went their separate ways. Apart from the other children, Billy loved school. He immensely enjoyed taking in information and creating. He was incredibly clever, more so than anyone realised, including him. In his early years, Billy's mother had nurtured his remarkable intelligence, but now she had to hold down multiple jobs. Billy was creative, more than most children his age. Creativity and reading, especially about nature, helped him calm down in a world so full of noise and clutter, a world he was trying to find his place in, but had always made him feel like an alien...like he didn't belong. He felt more comfortable with nature and animals than he did with people. In fact, he sort of resembled an animal his sister once told him. She said he looked like a meerkat twitching and looking around all the time.

He also had a strange birthmark on the top of his left arm. It just looked weird according to his sister, but Billy saw it as a brown splat, a sign of his creativity. The children at school used it as more ammunition to be mean to him, but he still liked it. It reminded him of a tattoo, even if it was brown. If he remembered correctly his mother had a large birthmark too.

As usual. Billy spent the entire school day trying to keep his head in books until the final bell rang out. At the end of the day, he picked up his sister and they made the slow tracks home. As they exited through the school gates, Billy thought he heard a crow cawing, but he couldn't see anything. Not that it was a problem; it would only be a second crow.

"Can you hear the bird cawing?" he asked Jessica. She strained to listen above the voices of the children and parents leaving the school.

"I hear a bird, but not nice tweeting. Where's it coming from?" she asked.

"I don't know. I can't see it anywhere. I think it's a crow."

"Crows are black aren't they, Billy?"

"Yes, they're black with a green or purple sheen," he replied.

This was Billy's opportunity to share his wealth of knowledge he'd gained in recent days. When the nightmares began, Billy delved into finding out as much as he could about birds.

"So I need to look for a black bird with shiny green or purple?" asked Jessica.

"Yes, but a crow is much greener than a rook's gloss, which is another black bird."

"Is it big or small?"

"Big, but smaller than a rook."

"How will I know the difference?"

"Crows beaks look shorter because of the curving down and they have a small patch of bristly feathers covering their nostrils, whereas a rook's beak is bare."

"Oh, OK." Jessica skipped away along the path. They weren't far away from their flat, which was round the back of the school.

A few moments later and they were in the cool of their flat, out of the summer sun.

"Jess, go change out of your school uniform straight into pyjamas," he told his sister. He did the same thing. Their mother asked them to do this to try to make the school uniforms last longer.

Jessica played with dolls in the living room. Billy looked out of the window. Something caught his eye.

Suddenly, a sparrow hit the window and Billy jumped back.

"Hey! You nearly landed on me," Jessica said.

"Sorry."

Jessica returned to her dolls. The kamikaze sparrow wasn't the strangest thing. Outside, Billy counted no less than forty-eight birds. Some perched on rooftops, in trees, on fences, and a few even wandered around on the tops of parked cars. Billy could have sworn they were staring at him. It gave him an uncomfortable feeling in the pit of his stomach.

"Don't be silly, Billy!" he mumbled to himself. "You don't mean anything to birds."

An overactive imagination wasn't always a blessing to Billy. He looked up to the blue sky instead. As he did so the school roof, not far from him, caught his attention. From a distance the roof looked like it had a rim covered in a shiny black oil slick. As he looked more intensely and it came into focus, Billy could see it was moving, but not like liquid.

"Oh my goodness!" he cried as he realised with horror what he saw. The roof was covered in birds; a majority were crows. There must have been hundreds of birds, all looking in his direction. The uncomfortable feeling in his stomach became a feeling of dread.

"Run, Jess!"

There was no movement behind him. He heard a scream come from their bedroom. He charged into the room. Winged creatures, including bats, filled the space round Jessica's bed where she sat screaming. They cawed and screeched loudly at Jessica.

One of the crows edged forward towards her. It began to grow larger and larger until it was the size of a man. The wings spanned half the room. From behind, Billy could see that the giant crow had huge scaly clawed feet. Black fabric cloaked its head and draped over the body.

As the crow morphed, it approached Jessica. Billy broke out of the shock trance he'd been in. He raced to his sister's side and threw himself on top of her.

"No, not her! Take me!" he screamed at the demented figure without looking up. He screamed the words over and over. Again the winged beast's caws shrieked.

Suddenly, Billy heard the window smash to his right. He refused to look up. The beasts squawked and shrilled loudly in distress as another bird sound was heard over the top of them. It was a mixture between a bark and a yelp.

Behind him, Billy could hear the flapping of feathers and items in his bedroom crashing on the floor and smashing against the walls. He felt the scratching of claws over his back and yelled out in pain. He still refused to look up so that he always covered his sister.

Squawking and slashing noises continued to fill the space around him. Then he heard the flapping and cawing move over to the window. The other newest winged creature squawked louder and Billy had to hold onto the bed frame to stop from blowing away from Jessica as he felt the gust of wind as this creature, which seemed bigger than the crow man, flapped its wings. He desperately wanted to see, but he couldn't...he wouldn't turn around.

"Argh!" he screamed, "Get off me!"

Beaks pecked at his entire body and pulled at his clothes and hair. Jessica was quietly crying beneath him. His body was aching as he tried to shield her without crushing her under his entire weight. He was propping himself up on different parts of his body as needed.

The noise began to die away until all he could hear was the whooshing wind of the larger creature.

After some time the room fell silent. Billy took a moment to peek behind him around the room. It was empty. Billy slowly pushed himself off of Jessica, who still sobbed silently with her eyes tight shut.

"It's OK, they're gone, Jess. It's safe." He looked around the room. There was nothing smashed or broken. Even the window, old and brittle as it was, was still in one piece in the frame. There was no damage at all. Not one thing was out of place.

Billy stood himself at the side of Jessica's bed. His barefoot landed on something both soft and hard. He lifted his foot. Stuck to the bottom of his foot was a black feather that glistened purple and green in the light. It was longer than his foot.

He ran to the window to look out. There was no crow to be seen. But, there on the windowsill, caught in the bottom of the net was a beautiful white feather. Billy picked the feather up. As he studied it he could see it was brown towards the hollow shaft.

Jessica came and flung her arms around her brother's waist. "What happened, Billy?"

"I don't know, Jess," he replied tucking the white feather into his pyjama waistband.

Chapter Two
Webbed Feet

It took Billy a long time to calm his little sister down. She was still snivelling. "I'm going to put the dinner on, Jess." He told her knowing she was hungry and food would make her feel better.

"OK," she croaked, her throat hoarse from so much crying, "What are we having?"

"Beans on toast...as usual." Neither of them were particularly pleased, but they had to eat, and beans on toast was better than nothing. They couldn't even have butter on the toast. With dinner Billy served them both glasses of tap water, juice was another luxury they couldn't afford. *Jess was right,* he thought, *it makes you wonder how many hours a person has to work just to afford a simple luxury like butter. His mother already worked every hour under the sun except weekends...was she supposed to work them too?*

"Go brush your teeth," Billy said once they had eaten up, "and make sure you wipe the bean juice off your face." He winked at Jessica, who responded by wiping her mouth with the back of her hand. She looked at the orange smudge on her hand.

"Got it!" she said.

Jessica went to the bathroom and Billy rinsed the plates and left them in the sink. He waited in their bedroom sitting to one side of Jessica's bed with a book open on his lap.

The floorboards in the hallway were so old they creaked even under Jessica's weight on her way to the bedroom. Billy could hear her gentle footsteps swiftly coming towards him and then Jessica burst into the room. The door hinges creaked too, and the door clanged against the wall. Another dusting of plaster fell from the wall where the door hit the same place repeatedly.

"You've got to stop that, Jess!" Billy said firm but kind.

"I don't mean to. I was hurrying because I was scared

on my own." She tip toed quickly to his side and clambered over him to get into bed. She snuggled down the bed resting her head on her pillow and leaning against the side of Billy. Billy had already flung back the duvet as it was a warm night and he gently covered her in only a bed sheet.

"Billy, stay with me tonight, I don't want to be on my own." Jessica used her cutest voice. She needn't have bothered; Billy wasn't leaving her alone tonight.

"I won't Jess." He stroked her hair and kissed her head. "I'll read to you and then I'll go to my bed and watch over you, OK?"

Jessica beamed up at him with that heart melting toothy smile. "OK, read," she ordered nudging the book open slightly.

"Once upon a time there was a beautiful little girl, nearly as beautiful as Jessica – "

"It doesn't say that!" Jessica protested.

"Hey! Who's reading this, you or me?" he jested.

"You," she said, "but it doesn't," she mumbled.

Billy quietly chuckled. "The beautiful girl lived in a high tower, and she desperately wanted to be outside in the world, in nature..."

Billy had barely got halfway through the story before

he could hear Jessica softly snoring. He quietly closed the book and slowly got up from the bed.

Billy lay in his own bed, not as eager to fall asleep as his sister after the events of the day. *What was to say the crow men wouldn't return in the dead of night?* Billy tried to stay awake, but rubbing his eyes just made them heavier. He was asleep within half an hour.

Billy stirred the following morning without the help of the neighbours blaring music. A shaft of light shone across his face and drool trickled on his chin. It must have been a very hot night as he'd kicked his bed sheet down to the bottom of his bed where his duvet cover lay crumpled.

Billy used to look forward to the weekends. His mother didn't work weekends. They were supposed to be for the family, but they never were. Billy gave up a long time ago on doing family activities. He used to be mad at his mother. He used to feel let down at how many times she broke a promise to take them out, but he was no longer mad and she no longer made promises. Besides, his mother needed the rest, her work exhausted her.

Billy got his clothes out of the wardrobe he shared with his sister and left the room.

In the bathroom, he freshened up. He pulled his faded

denim jean shorts on and a dishevelled red t-shirt. He looked in the mirror. His golden curls fell messily on his head. *Good job I like the bed head look...it's the only look my hair gives me!*

Billy may have slept well, but his reflection still showed the dark crescents he'd grown accustomed to seeing under his eyes. "That will do..."

He went into the living room. His mother had once again fallen asleep on the couch in her work uniform. This one was a green t-shirt with a name badge that read 'TRISH' and black trousers. Her black shoes had been kicked off and sprawled on the floor.

"Good morning, Mum," whispered Billy and he gave her a peck on the cheek. She exhaled deeply, but didn't wake.

"Billy!" Jessica appeared in the doorway.

"Shhh! Mum's sleeping." He pushed her back out of the room and closed the living room door.

"What are we doing today?"

"Get ready and I'll take us swimming," he replied. Jessica skipped off merrily.

Twenty minutes later, Billy was walking along the street watching Jessica drag a stick along garden fences.

Suddenly, Jessica stopped and bent down, "Look at

this, Billy!" she held up a feather. Billy swallowed. She held up a black feather in her little white hand. "I had a bad dream about birds last night. You called the main one a crow," she said.

"Aww, did you?" *A dream?* He thought.

"Yes, and you protected me from all these monsters and birds and bats. Well...not real you, because it was a dream." She dropped the feather again.

"What makes you think it was a dream?" Billy asked curious but happy she believed it to be a nightmare.

"Because in the dream, the room got destroyed and I heard the window smash, but it was tidy, as if by magic, when I opened my eyes...and magic is only for stories. That's what Mum says anyway."

"I guess you're right. Although, magicians do magic; not just witches and wizards...are magicians only in stories? Is their magic real? You even saw one when we had a show at school this year."

Jessica scratched her head, these were deep questions for a five year old, "Hmm, I'll have to think," she replied.

The conversation had passed the time and they were then standing in front of the glass doors of the swimming baths.

Ordinarily, there's no way they could have afforded to go swimming, but Mr Scott worked at the reception.

Mr Scott was one of their neighbours. He was quite a big guy and had what Billy's mother called 'a beer belly'. He had a shiny head and a brown bushy beard. Billy always thought it was funny having no hair on his head but hair on his chin. It was like Mr Scott's head was upside down. But Billy didn't laugh at Mr Scott, because Mr Scott was incredibly kind.

Mr Scott had taken pity on Billy and Jessica a few years ago. He knew their mother worked long hours and had seen Billy trying to keep his little sister occupied, which became harder once she could walk and didn't need a pushchair. Those days were easy; he'd roll her to the local library and read the books he liked to her. Jessica's mind wasn't like Billy's. She wanted to do something other than sit in a library and Mr Scott had overheard her complaining about just this several times.

Billy recalled Mr Scott's kind gesture on one occasion: Jessica was whining about wanting to do something, maybe a year ago, once she started hearing what other children in her class got up to on weekends and after school. Billy tried his best to explain their financial situation without everybody hearing, but Mr Scott had.

"Billy, is everything OK?" Mr Scott asked.

"Um, yes, Mr Scott," replied Billy. Jessica folded her arms and said nothing.

"You don't look very happy young lady." Mr Scott smiled at Jessica.

"I'm not! I'm bored!" she replied still stropping.

"You kids should go swimming on a hot day like today –"

"Oh yes! I think I'd like swimming," interrupted Jessica.

"Of course you would!" agreed Mr Scott brightly.

"Of course we would," agreed Billy sadly, "but we can't go." Billy looked at the floor.

"Oh, that's a shame," said Mr Scott, "I guess I'll have to give these lifetime free passes to two other children, eh?"

Jessica squealed with delight as Mr Scott produced two plastic cards with their names on. There was a blue splash on the card that read 'Tadpoles and Toads Club Member'.

"Tadpoles and Toads?" questioned Billy scrunching up his face.

"Yep," replied Mr Scott, "children and adults like to swim, don't they?"

Billy relaxed his face, "Yes, I guess they do."

Billy smiled as he recalled the day they received the swimming passes.

Jessica was waiting by the card-scanning machine. "Quick Billy!" she bounced excitedly.

Billy held out her card and Jessica pushed the barrier and then he scanned his own and followed her. They went to the family changing rooms.

After a few minutes both Billy and Jessica reappeared in their swimming costumes. Their mother had managed to save for them given the kind gesture by Mr Scott. Jessica wore a purple costume and Billy wore green and brown camouflage print shorts.

Jessica wasted no time jumping into the shallow end, and Billy jumped in after her, as she couldn't exactly swim yet! The water was cool and refreshing on his skin.

Billy was a natural swimmer. He felt free in the water. He loved how it held him. In the water the weight of the world slipped from his shoulders. Billy pulled Jessica around in the shallow end for a while and he let her ride on his back as he swam. She yelled and splashed with glee.

"I wish I could swim as well as you, Billy," she said.

"You will, if you practice," although Billy just seemed

to be able to swim on his first try.

"I want to start practicing now!"

"Now? You'll need a float."

"There's some over there." Jessica pointed to the other end of the pool by the edge, "let's go get one!" she threw herself into the water kicking her legs and flapping her arms and Billy swiftly held a hand under her to keep her afloat. They made their way to the edge of the pool and used the rail steps to get out.

"Mind how you go, it's slippery!" Billy called after her.

"I know!"

Jessica walked fast. As she rounded the corner of the deep end, she slipped and tumbled over the side of the pool and splashed into the water.

Billy didn't think; he reacted. He dived into the pool after her. He came up for air and saw his sister was still sinking. Bubbles were coming to the surface. He dived back under the water.

A weird sensation shot through his body and he gasped, swallowing water and returned to the surface before he drowned.

Jessica had sunk further and had nearly reached the bottom of the pool. He was surprised how quickly she was sinking.

He kicked his legs as hard as possible and seemed to glide much easier through the water. A few moments later he reached Jessica and tumbled around her so that he could push her to the surface rather than pull her. But, as he did so, he caught a glimpse of his legs, but they didn't look like his legs. They didn't look like anybody's legs! They weren't human! Sticking out of his shorts were legs that were similar in colour to his shorts...and at the end of those legs was a pair of webbed feet to match! Billy had to reach the surface with Jessica. He struck backward with his legs and the webbed feet opened creating a dam against the water. The strength of his leg muscles propelled him through the water. The larger surface area of his webbed feet applied more force against the surrounding water and he burst through the pool's surface in seconds. He treaded water until he reached the side and could push his sister onto the tiled edge. By the time he reached the side his legs had returned to normal.

"Thank goodness!" he exclaimed. The lifeguard had spotted them and was racing towards them ready to perform mouth-to-mouth resuscitation on Jessica, who lay unconscious, her chest still.

After a few attempts of chest compressions and

blowing air into her lungs, Jessica coughed and spluttered water.

"She's alive!" Billy said hugging her. The lifeguard moved Billy away and sat Jessica up.

"You gave us a scare little girl," he said. Jessica said nothing in response. "I'm going to get someone to look over her," he continued turning to Billy as he spoke.

By the time that Billy returned home with Jessica his mother was up and preparing a late lunch. Jessica ate and went for a nap, exhausted by the morning's events.

Billy and Mrs Wortol sat at the small kitchen table drinking a cup of tea. Billy sipped his, as it was too hot for him to swallow much like his mother did.

"How was swimming?" Mrs Wortol asked. Her voice seemed monotonous like she was filling the silence.

"Fine," he lied.

"Did you have fun?"

"Always do. I love swimming." He wasn't about to tell his mother that not only had her daughter nearly drowned but also he had magically grown toad or frog legs. She would think he was mad...anybody would!

"How about yesterday...did you have a good evening?"

"Yep," he lied again. There's no way she would believe

what happened yesterday either. *It was best not to say anything,* he thought.

Whilst he continued sipping his steaming tea, the doorbell rang. "I'll get it!" he said, eager to get away from the awkward situation. He pushed his chair away from the table.

Reaching the door he pulled it open. It stuck a little in the heat, but a big tug loosened it and it swung open slamming against the wall with a bang!

"What you doing out there?" yelled a disgruntled Mrs Wortol. Billy heard the scraping of her chair on the kitchen floor.

"Hello Billy," said the woman at the door. His mother looked at the lady on the doorstep and screamed at him, "Close the door! Close the door!"

Billy slammed the door in the woman's face startled by his mother's screaming.

"Get away from the door!" she barked at him and pulled him to her. It had been a long time since she'd held him. She looked like she'd seen a ghost. As she held him tight against her chest with her between him and the door, he could hear her heart racing.

"Mum, what's happening?" he didn't know what to expect after the last couple of days' events.

"Nothing," she lied. It seemed they had that in common.

"Who was that?"

"You don't need to know! You're to have nothing to do with her or any of them!" She was angry. Billy was actually almost pleased to see her show some kind of emotion.

The woman continued to knock on the door, in a strange melodious way. "You know that I can't leave without giving him the choice!" she called through the door. Her voice was quite deep for a woman.

"You'll not be talking to him!"

"You know I will. That's the rules, Patricia." The deep tones didn't terrify Billy like they seemed to terrify his mother. He found them quite pleasant, like a song.

"Mum, I don't understand...what –"

"Go to your room!" she pushed him towards his room, "Stay there!"

Mrs Wortol waited until she could see that Billy had gone into his room and had closed the door before she opened the front door to the mystery woman.

"He's not going with you!" she stated angrily.

The woman calmly replied, "He wouldn't start until September when the new academic year starts, so yes you're quite right: he's not coming with me...today."

They were unaware that Billy had cracked the door ajar and was listening to the conversation. *Were they talking about him?*

"He needs to know, Patricia. The key to the kingdom is his and it's his choice to take it or not and his alone. If he wants to join the academy or not, he must say."

"But –"

"He will be giving up a lot if he turns it down. You were given the same choice and so was his father. You both have keys to the kingdom."

Billy's heart beat faster at the mention of his father. He'd not been spoken about in years.

"He's not manifested anyway, maybe he doesn't need to attend," said Mrs Wortol, less confidently than before.

"You know that's not how the giving of the keys works. Manifesting now would be remarkable anyway." She exhaled deeply. "And are you sure he hasn't?"

"He hasn't said anything."

"But have you asked him?" asked the strange woman.

"Well, no, I haven't."

"We know he's bright. We knew that shortly after he was born. He probably realises he doesn't fit into the world around him, that something about him is different.

Don't you remember how you felt?"

"Yes, but things are different now. I no longer manifest and I never use my key."

"It doesn't mean you can't." The woman's voice was kind and she spoke in a tone that Billy had imagined the wise men of old had spoken that he'd read about in books.

"I won't!" The anger came back to her voice.

"That's your choice...just like this is Billy's choice."

Billy stepped out of his room and closed the door behind him so as not to disturb Jessica.

"What's my choice, Mum?" he asked, "What's she talking about? Who is she?"

Mrs Wortol was stunned to silence.

The woman stepped forward into the house. She turned to Billy's mother, "It's time to tell him." His mother stepped aside and let the woman enter.

Billy could see she wore peculiar attire. She had short white hair with silver tips. She wore a white pinstriped suit and a silver velvet crush shirt sat underneath the waistcoat matching the silver pinstripes. Her shoes were pointy, pointier than any shoes Billy had ever seen. And to finish the bizarre look off: upon her head was a silver top hat.

"I'm Miss Leadbetter and I'm the Headmistress at The Gifted Academy, which your mother attended." Mrs Wortol sighed deeply and hung her head.

"I'm here to present you with a key to the kingdom. We take on young warriors as students to grow their unique gifts. Has anything strange happened lately?" She winked at him, her eyes twinkled.

Billy was hesitant to answer truthfully. His mind had skipped over the warrior remark. He looked down at the floor, a habit he had anyway to avoid eye contact.

"My legs changed to frog or toad legs when I was swimming this morning," he blurted out still not looking up. *Why did he tell her that?*

"Ah, yes, *remarkable*!" said Miss Leadbetter, giving Mrs Wortol a sideways glance.

Miss Leadbetter proceeded to roll up her sleeve and then turned over her arm to reveal her forearm. There on her forearm was a large brown birthmark in the shape of a feather. "Now...let me see yours."

"How do you know I have one?" Billy asked.

"Call it a ...gift," she replied smiling.

Billy raised the sleeve baring the top of his left arm and there Miss Leadbetter and his mother could both see the mark. "It looks like a splat," said Billy.

Miss Leadbetter chuckled. "It's a mix, but I definitely see a toad print, to match your gift, possibly a feather too" she responded, "like your father... I assume." She looked at Mrs Wortol who blushed at the reminder but neither confirmed or denied it. Billy's eyes opened wide.

"You are a warrior, dear Billy, a key to the kingdom is awaiting you. If you choose to attend The Gifted Academy, we can hone your gifts, but if you choose not to ...you also forfeit the gift. But, like I said to your mother earlier: the choice is yours to make."

Billy looked at his mother who said nothing.

"I want to find where I belong, Mum. I want to go."

His mother breathed out slowly and choked back a sob, and her eyes glistened with tears.

"Here," Miss Leadbetter handed him an ornate brass key. "This is yours. Keep it on your person at all times and keep it safe. I suggest you don't start showing it to everyone." She clearly didn't know that he had no one to show it to. "I will be back for him the day term starts." And with that, Miss Leadbetter pivoted and left the flat. Billy hadn't even mentioned the crow man and was wondering whether he ought to have done. A conversation for another day now.

Chapter Three
Two Worlds

The summer dragged by for Billy. He had to contain his excitement because his mother still refused to talk about The Gifted Academy.

The first day of term would be 1 September. Quite early on the first of the month, excitement bubbling in his tummy, (or anxiety, he couldn't tell which), he ran to his mother who for once was awake on the sofa. He stumbled and stubbed his toe on the corner of the couch, "Stupid couch!" He mumbled." Mum, what do I need to pack? She's coming today!"

"Nothing," said Mrs Wortol.

Billy stopped in his tracks, "I'm still going aren't I?"

"Yes, but you don't need to take anything. You'll get it there."

"So, I just need to get ready to go? That's it?"

"Yes, Billy," she replied. Billy went to walk back to his room - "Billy," she called to him. He stopped. He turned back to face her. Her red hair hung loosely over her shoulders and the grey crescents under her eyes showed that life was taking its toll, but she was still beautiful. It was her eyes; they sparkled with kindness and crows feet formed when she smiled.

"Yes, Mum?"

She placed her hands on his shoulders and bent down so that she looked him in the eyes. It hurt her back as he was quite small for his age and she'd been stacking groceries all night long so that she could be home when he left. She smiled at him, filling him with warmth, "You know you can change your mind at any time while you're there? You can always come home."

"I know, Mum," he threw his arms around her neck and she squeezed him so tight and for so long he wasn't sure she would ever let go. He didn't care at that moment. It had been a long time since she'd shown such an emotion.

She let go and stood straight. Her lower back clicked.

"Run along and get ready. She'll be here soon. He ran off to get dressed. His mother called after him, "Don't forget your breakfast and to brush your teeth!" Billy had taken care of his own breakfast and brushing his teeth for a long time, and his sister's for that matter, but it felt kind of nice being treated like a child...after all...he was one.

Half an hour later the doorbell rang. "I'll get it!" yelled Billy, sprinting for the door and nearly taking out his sister in the process. She just managed to move out of his way. Jessica followed him to the door, followed by Mrs Wortol. Billy opened the door.

"Good morning, Billy. Ready?" The deep voice of Miss Leadbetter soothed his churning stomach.

"Morning, Miss Leadbetter." He turned to look at his mother and sister, "Yes, I'm ready."

"I want to go with Billy!" whined Jessica wrapping herself around his waist.

Mrs Wortol started to pull Jessica away – "Wait!" said Billy. He bent down to his sister and whispered in her ear. She stepped back and hugged her mother's leg, smiling.

"What did you say to Jess?" asked Mrs Wortol.

"It's a secret," replied Jessica on Billy's behalf. She showed that goofy grin of hers.

Billy gave his mother one last hug before turning and walking away with Miss Leadbetter.

They walked along his road in silence for about two minutes, until Miss Leadbetter broke the silence "You'll be fine, Billy, and so will they."

Billy breathed deeply. "I know," he said, "It just feels strange leaving Jess. And I don't know what to expect."

"Expect the unexpected!"

Billy didn't know what to make of her statement and changed the subject, "How are we getting there?"

"You'll see when we get just around that corner." She pointed to the upcoming corner on the left, about a hundred paces along the road. Billy wondered what would be there. Miss Leadbetter's statement floated through his mind 'expect the unexpected'. *What on earth would it be? A motorbike. No unlikely, neither of them were dressed appropriately for that. A car? But that's not unexpected. A fancy one? A Rolls Royce? Or a convertible maybe? Oh, maybe a limousine, Miss Leadbetter did dress pretty fancy, strange, but definitely fancy. It couldn't be a train because there were no stations nearby. Equally it couldn't be a boat because there were no rivers nearby.*

As they rounded the corner Billy heard their mode of

transport before he saw it. Snorting and neighing filled the air of the quiet, dead end road. The road was lined with houses. At the end was a park that led to woodlands. It wasn't a particularly long road. The horse was waiting by itself at the park gate. Billy pointed at it, his eyes wide and hopeful. "That? We're going by horse?" Miss Leadbetter chuckled. "Yes," she replied. "Pleased?"

"Yes! Very much so! Can I touch it?"

"Yes, but be careful, Mr Shore isn't too fond of being petted."

"Mr Shore? That's an odd name for a horse. Although, a lot of 'odd' stuff has been happening lately, so I don't know why I'm surprised." Billy ran towards the horse listening to Miss Leadbetter laughing behind him.

As Billy stood next to the horse, he felt even smaller than usual. It was at least twice his height. He stroked the side of the magnificent animal. Its chestnut fur shimmered in the sunlight. Its beautiful brown mane blew in the summer breeze. Billy walked the entire way around the horse taking in its swishing tail, its long muscular legs and looking into its dark chocolate eyes. He reached a hand up to touch its face—

"I wouldn't do that if I were you!" Miss Leadbetter called out as the horse pulled its head out of reach. Billy let his hand drop and stood back by the horse's side where he'd started.

"You said I could touch it."

"Yes, but maybe not his face; Mr Shore would not stand for that and I'll only have to hear about it later."

Billy was completely baffled by many of Miss Leadbetter's remarks. He thought it best that he just got used to it.

"OK. How do we ride it?" Billy asked, "It has no saddle."

"Mr Shore is a 'he' and we ride him bareback of course!"

"Of course..." mumbled Billy, not sure what was so obvious about riding a horse bareback.

Miss Leadbetter suddenly threw herself onto the horse's back, which neighed and huffed. "Be quiet Mr Shore, I'm not that heavy. Don't be cheeky!"

She turned and grinned at Billy. "Give me your hand," she ordered. Billy lifted his hand towards her. She grabbed it and swung him easily onto the horse's back behind her. "Hold on to me tightly, Billy! Here we go!"

Billy gripped his arms around her waist. She held the horse's mane shouting, "Mr Shore, go!"

The horse took off at a swift trot into the park. The

trot quickly turned to a gallop. They were heading for the woodlands, with no intention of slowing down apparently, thought Billy. He lent into Miss Leadbetter, scared of being hit with branches as they whizzed through the woodland. Twigs and leaves scratched at his arms but no real pain or damage was done.

The horse's hooves thudded on the dirt, dried out by a summer of no rain. Dust kicked up into the air. The horse began to move so fast that the trees became a blur of brown and green smudges. Billy couldn't even talk; the wind made his cheeks flap.

All of a sudden white light swirled with the green and brown blur. Billy was forced to close his eyes for fear of getting dizzy and vomiting. It was probably a good job he couldn't open his mouth – it could keep the vomit from escaping! Only when he felt the horse dramatically slowing down did he dare to open his eyes. When he did, he was awestruck.

They were going down a dirt track with great oak trees on either side, but there were no tracks like this one in the woodlands connected to the park. *Where were they?*

As they trotted along at a much more comfortable pace (as afar as Billy was concerned) he could hear the beating of drums in the distance, mixed with roars of laughter and shouting.

As he got closer he could distinguish between adults and children's voices and delicious smells filled the air. They reminded him that he hadn't eaten a big breakfast. His stomach rumbled. He wasn't sure if it was safe for him to eat so soon after the flips the journey had made his stomach do. Probably best for him to leave it some time before he ate.

The wooded area began to lighten as they drew nearer to the music and smells. Mr Shore suddenly stopped. "This is where we stop our ride!" Miss Leadbetter leapt from the horse's back and landed gracefully like a gymnast. "Here, let me help you down." She stood sideways on so that Billy could lean on her shoulder and jump to the ground. His legs buckled a little. "They'll soon get better, don't you worry," she said.

She turned to the horse, "Thank you for a safe trip, Mr Shore. You're job is done."

Before Billy's eyes, the horse reared up onto its hind legs and began to shrink. Its fur began to fade away and cotton fabric appeared. Fingers, then arms and finally the face of the horse morphed into a man. He shook his head and his long brown wavy hair fell into place down his back, coincidently as a ponytail. He was dressed fairly similar to Miss Leadbetter, in that it was strange. A moss green bowler hat upon his head matched the corduroy trousers, and cotton shirt. But a brown velvet tie hung between the lapels of a tailored velvet milk chocolate blazer.

Billy's mouth opened so wide with shock that his jaw felt like it had hit the floor. The man gave a throaty laugh and his bearded jaw quivered.

"Billy, let me introduce you to Mr Shore, another member of The Gifted Academy's staff. He teaches English and does enjoy to make things more dramatically than necessary."

Mr Shore held his hand out for Billy to shake. Billy took it gently, still bewildered, "Hello, Billy."

"H-hi," Billy stammered. "Now I know why you had a human name as a horse."

"Don't be so sure that logic will work for you in this place."

"Where are we?" Billy asked.

"Follow me," said Miss Leadbetter. She led Billy out of the woods into the opening. The noise was overwhelming. So many people bustled about. Most people were dressed equally as weird as Mr Shore and Miss Leadbetter. In fact, looking around Billy could see it was only children dressed a little more normal.

"This is the local market place situated closest to The Gifted Academy," said Miss Leadbetter. "This is Greenacre."

"Greenacre," mumbled Billy as he turned on the spot taking in as much as he could.

They walked into the market place and needed to speak louder as they passed the musicians playing stringed instruments and ladies and gentlemen danced in groups to the cheerful music. Markets back home were never that exciting.

Everywhere he looked were tents, like he once saw for the circus. They all looked like variations of the Big Top. Large white and blue striped ones, red and green ones, so many it looked like a tent city. Also, there were brightly coloured ropes fastened to large wooden pegs in the grass.

Stalls filled the entrances of the tents selling animals, food, and instruments among a whole load of amazing things. They were passing them all.

"What are we doing here, Miss Leadbetter?"

"We need to get you kitted out for the academy. Now, don't panic, I have plenty of your father's money."

"You do?" Billy looked down at his worn out trainers

that had holes in the soles and the faded t-shirt. He thought back to how he, his mother and Jessica had been living on next to nothing, when there was so much of his father's money there.

Miss Leadbetter looked at Billy's sad face. She knew how he'd been living. It was no secret in this world what Mrs Wortol had become in the other world.

"Dear, she couldn't use it there." She lifted his chin with one finger to look him in the face.

"Use what?" Billy decided to play dumb.

"The money, Billy. The money here is only any use here; not there. It wouldn't have given you any better a life back home."

Billy didn't know whether to feel relieved or embarrassed that Miss Leadbetter clearly knew the situation at home. *Was it that obvious?*

"Let's get you clothed appropriately, like the other year sevens." That's when Billy noticed the adults around him holding various items of fabric: velvet, wool, silk, cotton and others, up to their children.

"Are they here with their parents?" asked Billy.

"Yes, most of them, or some form of guardian."

"Oh," he said sadly, "So why didn't my mum come with me?"

"I can't speak for her, Billy, but I can tell you she's not been here for very many years." She paused and stared off into the distance remembering. "But enough of that for today."

"Mother, I want that one!" One black haired boy was screaming at his mother pointing at an elaborate white silk tunic with gold lace embroidery. It looked incredibly expensive.

"Fine, Sweetheart, if that's what you want." She paid the seller with gold and silver lumps. They looked like sort of glass nuggets.

Miss Leadbetter bent down and spoke quietly into Billy's ear, "Just because it's expensive, doesn't mean the quality matches the price." She gave him a friendly nudge and a wink.

A few tents along and Miss Leadbetter stopped in front of another clothing stall with quality items at a lower cost. Billy didn't really understand how the money worked there yet.

"OK, Billy, you need to choose something with blue in it to represent water, which will be your House in the academy."

"Why water?" asked Billy.

"Your animal so far is an amphibian of some sort, and

they are put in Water House, which is blue. Although, that might change, but I hope for your sake it doesn't." Billy didn't ask any more questions. It would probably only confuse him further.

Billy picked out several tunics, jackets, trousers, shoes, shirts and accessories all with a hint of blue, even if it was only a button or two.

During his clothes picking time Miss Leadbetter wandered off. When she returned she held a spherical glass bowl with a wire mesh lid. "You'll be needing this," she said plonking it in Billy's arms. She proceeded to pay for his clothes handing over several glass nuggets of different colours.

"It's empty," said Billy looking into the bowl.

"Of course it's empty!" There she was making those implications of his obvious statements again.

"OK, lets move on. I'll take you round the next few stalls." Miss Leadbetter led Billy around the stalls picking up textbooks for English, maths, science and various other normal ones much to his delight. He also picked out an instrument for his music class. He chose a lovely blue wood grain guitar.

Billy was beginning to think that maybe the academy wouldn't be so weird after all...until Miss Leadbetter handed him a bow and arrow set and some kind of fake leather armour (it must have been fake because it did not smell like leather). "Thought you'd prefer the bow to a sword."

As she handed them to him, he fumbled and dropped the arrows, scattering them over the grass. He quickly bent to pick up what he could.

"Here," a dark-brown-skinned boy with short black tight curls handed him a couple of arrows. Billy noticed he was dressed in normal clothes still: jeans and t-shirt, just like him.

"Thanks," he said taking the arrows and placing them back in his quiver.

"I'm Jacob." He held out a clammy hand with long fingers. He was quite a bit taller than Billy. Billy shook his hand energetically, grateful that he might make a friend. This place was already better than home if that happened.

"Billy."

"You starting at The Gifted Academy this year?"

"Um, yeah I am."

"Do you know what House you're going to be in?"

"Water, I think Miss Leadbetter said."

"Whoa! You've met the Headmistress already? She's supposed to be really cool...not like my old one 'Mrs

Cabbage'. I couldn't wait to come here, it's supposed –"

Billy interrupted before they got too far off topic, "What House are you in?"

"Water. Hey! We could bunk together? But until we're checked there's always the possibility of change.

Billy had no idea where they would be bunking but this boy seemed pleasant enough.

A drum roll sounded loudly and continually over all the music.

"Hey! That's for us, we've gotta meet over by the jugglers and get ready to walk to the academy." Jacob threw a large rucksack onto his back, which was jam-packed and a few other bags. "Where's your stuff?"

Miss Leadbetter came over from the seller. She'd seen the boys talking and had given them space. It was about time Billy made a friend and a 'Sole' boy wasn't a bad choice. She loaded Billy up with his bags and hooked his glass bowl to his rucksack.

"What's that?" asked Jacob poking the bowl with a long finger.

"I don't know yet."

"You know it's empty right?"

"Yes," said Billy. He laughed and Jacob joined in. Jacob led the way to where other children waited. All with rucksacks bigger than themselves, but none carrying a large glass bowl, thought Billy.

Miss Leadbetter made her way to the front and had been joined by Mr Shore and several other adults. They started walking and the crowd of year sevens started following.

They went, once again, into the woodland. Billy loved the smell of the bark. He loved nature and this place was truly nature at its best. Greens seemed greener and browns richer, earthy smells more fragrant.

Billy heard a bird chirping, in a tree overhead. He looked up to see what it was and tripped over a rock, face-planting the pathway and skidding. He winced. Jacob helped him up, "You alright, Mate?"

"My face hurts." He touched his face and winced more. It was not the time to cry. A little blood came away on his fingers.

"You've grazed your jaw along the right hand side," said Jacob, "Looks painful, Mate."

"It is."

The blonde girl in front of them didn't carry on walking with the rest of the children when Billy fell. She ran up to him. Her eyes were a beautiful blue behind thick black-framed glasses. Her long hair reached her elbows. "Can I see it?" She didn't wait for a response but put her face right in front of Billy's. "Are you hurt anywhere else?"

"Not really. My face took most of the fall."

"Can I..?" Without finishing her sentence she placed her hand over the graze on Billy's face. He expected excruciating pain, but instead was surprised by a warm soothing sensation. "There, all done." When she removed her hand, Billy saw Jacob's eyes nearly pop out of his head.

"What?" asked Billy touching his face. No pain. He looked at his fingers. No blood.

"I have healing power. Only just started but it comes in useful...what I can do," she said.

"Thanks," said Billy incredibly grateful.

"You're welcome. I'm Malyssa." She didn't hold out a hand, which Billy preferred.

"I'm Billy."

"Jacob."

A cry came from the children who'd carried on, "Hang on everyone! The babies are falling behind. Little legs can't keep up!" A few other children around him laughed.

Malyssa called back, "He fell over," pointing at Billy. She meant it in defence of them falling behind, but the large blob of a boy used it against them.

"Oh dear! One of the babies fell over! Want to go home to your mummy?" He pulled a mock sad face.

"Ignore him," said Billy. He was more than used to bullies. "What House are you in?" Billy was hoping he used the correct lingo.

"Air," replied Malyssa. *Phew, got the word right,* thought Billy.

"We're both Water...probably," he said, "Although Miss Leadbetter and Jacob did say they could change."

'Why? The Birthmark books only tell you exactly what the mark is… narrow it down, Houses aren't normally completely changed."

"I don't know."

"What's your birthmark of?" Jacob asked him.

"Looks like a frog print, but it's not clear and –"

"Then, yes, you'll be in Water House –" said Malyssa.

"...And a feather, I think."

Jacob and Malyssa fell silent.

"Why have you gone quiet? What did I say?"

"You have two birthmarks, Billy," said Jacob.

"So? Why does it matter?" asked Billy, chasing it up quickly with, "Miss Leadbetter said my father had two."

Silence again. Jacob and Malyssa looked at each other.

"What am I missing?" Billy was confused and eager to know what they both knew.

"The only other person who had two birthmarks was 'The Beast'." Malyssa whispered the name.

"Who's The Beast?"

"He's an ex pupil of The Gifted Academy, but...he's pure evil. He stays alive over the centuries by taking on another body as a host," said Malyssa shuddering at the mere mention of him. "No-one's seen him for a while, but, we all know he's planning an attack at some point. Although, there was that *plummeting the world into darkness* business last year, which was attributed to him, but that's just rumoured."

"Well, it's not my father," stated Billy firmly.

"It's got to be, Mate," said Jacob, "There's only the two of you with the double birthmarks in the whole world."

"Well, there must be a third, because my father..." Billy gulped, he'd not said the next part of his sentence for a long time, if ever, "...my father...died...saving my life! And if you ask me, sacrificing himself for me is definitely not evil!"

Jacob and Malyssa were stunned. All three of them walked in silence for what felt like hours but was mere moments.

Malyssa broke the silence, "You're right, Billy, that's most definitely not evil. There must be a mistake in the records."

"Or maybe it's in secret records," said Jacob.

"Maybe," said Billy. He calmed down really quickly and couldn't believe these two were being so nice to him despite his outburst.

"Did-did you ever see your dad's birthmark, Billy?" asked Malyssa hesitantly.

"I don't think so, but if I did, I don't remember...I was only six when it happened." He looked down to the ground.

Jacob sensed the awkwardness, "So, we're nearly to the academy. I can't wait to see it for real. I've only seen photos. My sister says it's amazing!"

"Me too!" said Malyssa and Billy in unison.

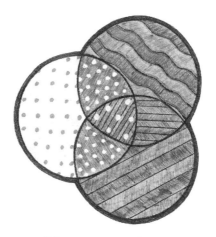

Chapter Four

Woodland Walk

"I don't really know anything about this place," said Billy.

"You been living under a rock?" joked Jacob.

"Might as well have been," mumbled Billy under his breath, but replied, "No, but until summer this year I'd never have believed any of this existed. I'd never heard of this sort of 'stuff' apart from in books."

"Where do you think the ideas come from, Mate? They don't just pluck them out of thin air!" He chuckled amazed at Billy's lack of understanding.

"So, all the authors in the other world know this place? Are they from here?"

"No, no, no," said Jacob, "But over the years people do get a glimpse and their imaginations run with it." He adjusted his rucksack on his back which was starting to get uncomfortable and continued, "But it's sad really, they usually only believe the stories to be...well...stories."

Billy looked around him at all the children with their bags, all the trees and plants and thoughts about the crow man and his frog legs. Part of him was still not sure that this wasn't an elaborate story or possibly a dream. Maybe he had fallen and bumped his head and things weren't quite right. But...everything seemed so real; especially when he hurt his face.

"Tell me more about this place. I mean, where are we?"

Malyssa piped up, "This is still England, up north, but it's in a different realm. Both realms occupy the same space at the same time, but only those 'gifted' can be part of both and go between the two."

"OK, that was actually clearer than I expected, thanks."

"I'm going to stop a minute, I need to put on a sweater or whatever they're called here. I'm getting chilly." He dropped his rucksack on the ground, undid the toggles at the top and expected to have to rummage but Miss Leadbetter had placed a cardigan on top. Billy had a sneaky suspicion Miss Leadbetter knew that he'd feel the drop in temperature in this realm and would need the easy access to a warmer item of clothing. He didn't know how she knew but he had this funny feeling deep within him that she did. In fact, he'd go as far as to assume she knew a lot more than most about most things.

He pulled a navy blue cardigan made of wool from his rucksack. He quickly pulled it over his head without undoing the sky-blue buttons, readjusted the toggles on his rucksack and with some help from Malyssa and Jacob, put his bag back on his back.

The three of them had fallen quite far behind the others and picked up the pace. Billy's empty glass bowl that was hooked to his rucksack banged loudly against the bag and sometimes against his arm.

Great, a weird birthmark on one arm and tomorrow I'll have a bruise on the other to match!

Suddenly, there was a loud rustle of leaves nearby. All three turned to face it, not sure what to expect.

"There's nothing there," said Malyssa relieved.

"Must have just been the wind through the trees," surmised Jacob.

Billy stared in the direction the noise had come from scrutinising every branch, twig and leaf. Recent unexpected events had taught him not to take things so lightly and Miss Leadbetter had told him to 'expect the unexpected'. But even he had to admit after focussed observation that he couldn't see anything. Maybe if there was something it had gone or was camouflaged. Something didn't feel right...or maybe he was paranoid. Jacob and Malyssa didn't seem bothered after all.

"What's the time? Feels like this day is lasting forever," asked Billy.

"By earthly time, it's about one o'clock –"

"– But time isn't really important in this realm," cut in Malyssa, more desperate to explain than Jacob. Cutting in was her only chance to be the one to explain.

"What do you mean it's not really important?"

Malyssa wiggled her nose like a rabbit and frowned searching for the right words, "This realm is outside of time."

"I don't follow. You don't have clocks...you don't have day and night? Because it's daytime now and it's certainly brighter than when I arrived this morning."

"This world mirrors the time of the earthly world. So, the best way to explain it is that; yes, there is time, for those of us who continue to mingle in the other world. So for instance, we will have times to be at our classes etcetera, but once we are out of the academy, if we choose to remain only in this world, and not work at an academy, then we don't need to worry about time." Malyssa tried to explain.

Billy's face gave away the fact that he was more confused than before!

"It's like this, Mate: no one dies here, you just keep going until you've reached the 'right' age for you and then you live forever at that age."

"No one dies? Then why are people scared of this man with the two birthmarks?"

Jacob put his palm to his forehead, feeling stupid for his mistake, "Sorry, I misspoke, no one dies naturally here, of say old age, because they stop aging, but –"

Malyssa interrupted again impatient with Jacob's slow speech, "– but we can be killed!"

Billy sighed deeply, "Lovely," he said less than pleased with this new information.

Everyone sensed the low mood Billy was now in contemplating information as they continued to drag themselves through the forest to wherever they were heading, which didn't seem to be ending, thought Billy, despite Jacob's earlier remark about nearly being there. Maybe he's already forgotten how time works, thought Billy sarcastically. He was getting irritable from hunger. *You'd think I'd be used to it by now!*

Malyssa changed the subject, "Let's talk about something happier. Sooo, how did you find out about this place? You said it was recent events."

Billy thought for a moment before answering, the memories flashing across his mind. "My sister and I were attacked at our home by birds and bats and anything else that could fly!"

"Not sure I understand how that told you about this place, Mate," said Jacob.

"Literally, in our home! In my and Jess' bedroom! Loads of them trying to get Jess!"

"Who's Jess?"

"My five year old sister. I shielded her. She thinks it was a bad dream, which is probably for the best, because..." he trailed off.

"Because of what?" urged Malyssa.

"Because of what happened next...I mean, I could probably explain a bunch of creatures coming in through the window if I had to, but the rest made no sense,"

Jacob and Malyssa looked at each other and then

stared back at Billy for the next part of the story.

"And then...then there was the crow. It grew and transformed into a hideous crow man!"

"A crow man!" They both exclaimed.

"That's someone from here!" cried Malyssa in shock.

"I can't believe it!" said Jacob.

"No-one's been attacked by another Manifestus in years!" added Malyssa. She looked at Jacob, "Do you think it's The Beast?"

"I doubt it, why would he go after Billy's sister as his first returning act?" The question stumped them, but helped them relax as they thought about the logic.

"How'd you get away?" asked Jacob, anxious to hear more.

"I didn't. Something came in and scared them all off."

"What was it?"

"I don't know but it was some kind of bird because I found a..." he reached into the waist band at the back of his shorts, "feather. But it's huge and not black, so it definitely doesn't belong to a crow." He passed it around to the others, "Either of you know what bird it's from?"

Jacob shrugged and passed it to Malyssa.

"I'm not sure," she said, "but you're right, it's got to be big."

Billy retrieved it and placed it back safely in his waistband. It tickled his back, which was pleasant considering how awkward it was twisting to get it between his body and bag.

"Question," said Malyssa, "how did you know that it was from here that the crow man came?"

"Oh, I guess I didn't then," he replied.

"So, there's more to the story?" asked Jacob.

"Um, yes." Billy told them about his experience at the swimming pool and his legs morphing into green frogs legs and how he saved his sister again.

"Wow!" cried Jacob and Malyssa. Billy noticed they kept exchanging glances. He assumed it was because he'd saved his sister's life... twice, "I'm sure you two would have done the same for your family," he said modestly.

Jacob and Malyssa looked at each other again. "Stop looking at each other like that please and explain what I said wrong."

"Nothing wrong," said Malyssa truthfully.

"So what is it then?" asked Billy.

"We can't believe you manifested before even starting the academy," explained Jacob, "No-one has ever done that in history as far as I know!"

"What was it like?"

"Weird...but so cool!" Billy was smiling now mirroring Jacob and Malyssa's excitement.

"So, you didn't manifest completely into a frog? It was just your legs?"

"My legs were all I noticed had changed, but..." he ran his fingers through his blonde curls and scratched his head, "I could hold my breath a lot easier and for longer."

"That's so cool!"

"You must be the youngest person ever to semi-manifest!" said Malyssa, tousling her own hair.

Billy frowned. "Wouldn't it be a better thing to have fully manifested?" he asked, "I was still human, for the most part."

"No!" exclaimed Jacob, "My sister says it's easier to morph into the actual animal than it is to control your body so that it only changes a part of it!"

"I thought I was going to be furthest along with the fact I can already use some of my power to heal, when I was flicking through my older brother's notes. I'm the same animal as him," she said proudly.

"What winged animal are you that you can heal?" asked Jacob trying to think and coming up empty.

"A bee."

"A bee?" he scoffed, "Bees sting people; that hurts not

heals!" He laughed, which irritated Malyssa.

"Actually, for your information, Clever Clogs, bees also make honey, which is used in many healing remedies!" She poked her tongue out at Jacob.

Billy was giggling at them. He couldn't believe how long these two had been talking with him. It was the longest conversation he'd had with other children that wasn't his sister!

Malyssa shot him a glance that stopped his giggling. "Anyway," she said, "that doesn't explain how you know this place...how'd you make the connection to here from those events?"

"Oh, I didn't, Miss Leadbetter showed up at my home and told me," he said matter-of-factly.

"What? She went to your House? Wow!"

"What's so shocking?"

"She doesn't make House calls normally! You're so lucky!"

"My mum didn't seem to think so. She didn't want to let Miss Leadbetter in our home. In fact, she didn't want me to come here." Billy glanced at his feet. The soles of his feet were hurting, the twigs and stones were digging in through the holes in the worn soles.

"Oh! That's why she was the one who handed you

your stuff...you already knew her and she knew it was your bag!" Jacob nodded his head pleased with himself.

"Actually, she brought me here...by horse."

"I can't believe it! This is crazy! Who are you?"

Good question, thought Billy. "The horse turned out to be Mr Shore."

Jacob could no longer contain his amazement; he held his head trying to soothe his mind before it exploded.

"I'm nothing special," Billy said, "think she had to come because my mum wouldn't have told me and there're rules apparently."

It can be tough for parents that aren't gifted –"

Billy interrupted, "She is gifted! She came here! Miss Leadbetter said so the first day!"

"Why wouldn't she want you to come here if she did?'

"I honestly don't know."

Suddenly, a trumpet sounded, startling all three of them again. Malyssa and Jacob quickly composed themselves and started cheering with everyone else in front, who they'd nearly caught up with by now.

"Ha ha! We're there!"

Billy looked around. Nothing. He squinted into the distance. Nothing. They were surrounded by forest, not a building in sight.

"There's nothing here."

Malyssa was laughing. "You'll see," she said.

The trumpet continued to sound and others joined in. Every child except Billy started cheering. He craned his neck to see past the other children. All he could see was a footbridge over a river that led to more forest.

The trumpeting stopped abruptly, followed by the children falling silent. All Billy could hear was the rushing river up ahead of them. Then he caught the faint sound of drums and as a cymbal clashed something came flying out of the river. Each time a cymbal crashed another 'something' splashed through the surface of the water.

Billy couldn't believe his eyes. He rubbed them, then continued to gawp as the scene was still there. "It makes no sense," he mumbled, but Malyssa heard him.

"What makes no sense?" She kept her eyes on the events before them.

"That was a crocodile, a-a dolphin, an orca! And look that's a shark!"

"So?" said Jacob, catching up with the conversation.

"They don't belong here or together." Billy was completely baffled. Malyssa and Jacob were laughing and waiting expectantly.

As they reached the footbridge a variety of large water

animals burst out of the river on both sides and arched over the bridge landing on opposite sides accompanied by ooos and ahs from the crowd.

Suddenly, Billy noticed Miss Leadbetter and the other teachers running forward, sprinting even. Billy felt a shot of panic fire through his entire body. He went to run too, but Malyssa grabbed his hand, "Just watch and walk." She was smiling, clearly not terrified.

Mr Shore manifested into the magnificent chestnut horse he'd been earlier and continued to gallop. Other teachers transformed into large wolves and foxes and a beautiful deer leapt over a log. They started to curve away leaving Miss Leadbetter running straight ahead by herself, until she leapt into the air and manifested into an awesome eagle. She swooped up and looped back on herself and was flying above the children who squealed in delight, she dipped passing over Billy, touching his hair with the tip of one of her wings before looping back.

Billy was so in awe of her he hadn't even noticed where they were approaching.

A bunch of boys and girls ahead of Billy started pointing and yelling, "Look, up there! Tops of the trees! There's another bird!"

It dived down in front of them and as it did, gates

appeared. They were nothing fancy. Just long planks of wood. But the gates no longer mattered. For as they approached them they opened slowly and the view beyond changed from the simple woodland they'd been walking through.

Ahead of them were log cabins, magnificent log cabins. They were more like log mansions.

"That's The Gifted Academy building!" exclaimed Jacob.

"We stay in there?" asked Billy disbelieving he was even awake.

"No, that's just where our lessons take place."

There were large wooden columns ornately decorated with carved wooden vines. Water whooshed through huge glass tunnels between different parts of the building. Beautiful spiralling staircases, wooden ladders and rope ladders leading to different floors. Billy could only see the front; he had no idea how far back it went.

"It's all made of wood, and some stone and glass?" he asked.

"Most of it," replied Malyssa, 'not a red brick in sight!"

"If this is what the outside looks like, I can't wait to check out the inside!"

"Tell me about it!" said Jacob.

Billy realised looking at the landscape that they hadn't passed over a river before, but part of a moat. It definitely seemed to curve round the building. Or at least he thought it did, he couldn't really see where the water went. Maybe he was getting carried away in the excitement.

They stopped at the foot of the stone steps leading to a set of wooden doors. The doors opened inwards, not a creak to be heard. Out between the double doors stepped Miss Leadbetter back in human form. Her top hat balanced just as well as before upon her head.

"OK, year sevens. When you go in drop your luggage in the entrance. Remember where you drop it, you don't want to waste time finding it and be last to your dormitories." She said this last bit in particular to a girl in the front who was staring out to the landscape, rather than listening, "Isn't that so, Blossom?"

The girl turned around to face Miss Leadbetter, her eyes wide with fear, but Miss Leadbetter kindly smiled in response.

Miss Leadbetter led the way through the double doors. Billy could over hear Blossom talking to those around her, "How does she know my name already?"

"She's amazing!" claimed another.

But the boy who teased Billy earlier turned round to his cronies and said, "She's a great loser! That's what she is! Look at her the weirdo! I don't know how the government kept her here after what she did last year!"

Miss Leadbetter stood before another set of double doors, but these ones were glass. Billy peered through the windows at the strange room. The rest of the academy was in there, already eating. The room was cylindrical and seemed to separate into thirds around a central round table, which seated the staff who sat looking outwards. He could see blocks of students dressed in blue in one area, green and brown in another and white and silver in yet another. That was surely not coincidence, he thought.

Four members of staff, including Miss Leadbetter, stood outside the room with large, worn books in their hands. One each.

"Please form four lines and be ready to expose your birthmark so that your team, or *House* if you will, can be determined.

The year sevens spread themselves out as directed.

Chapter Five
Birthmarks

Billy followed Malyssa and Jacob to the queue forming nearest them. Billy recognised the male teacher from the market place, but he hadn't been with them when they'd walked together to the academy, so how had he got there? Maybe there were other routes or certainly other ways to travel, thought Billy.

Billy prepared himself as Jacob exposed his own shin to the male teacher revealing his birthmark. Billy's, being on the top of his arm, practically his shoulder, was more difficult to reach with his cardigan on, and despite the fact that it was much cooler inside the building, he had to remove his cardigan.

He managed to get it off of his head just in time to hear the teacher talking to Jacob, "looks like a little goldfish," he said loud enough for everyone to hear, "So you're in Water."

"Goldfish!" exclaimed Jacob with embarrassment and disbelief.

The brutish boy they'd met earlier that day laughed so much he was practically coughing, "Goldfish! What a joke! Little fish!"

Jacob was annoyed, he turned to the teacher, "How on earth can you tell it's a goldfish? You didn't even look in the book!"

"Despite your audacity to speak to me like that, Jacob Sole, I will answer your question, to put your mind at ease." He flicked open the brown leather-bound book in his arms and immediately found a shape entitled 'goldfish'. There, clear as day, was a match for Jacob's sign, "A very common sign back in the day, Jacob." He closed the book with a snap. "Move along and do not question my authority again." He spoke in a low, deep voice. He ran a hand over his dark, baldhead, "Next!"

It was Malyssa's turn. She stepped up to him revealing her right ankle. She was shaking a little, but enough that Billy could see it. "Obviously, insect. Let me check which one." He opened the book again mumbling as he did so, "not that there's much use in having an insect in my House among great flying birds and bats."

He wasn't quiet enough. Malyssa heard every word and close to tears ran for the group of children wearing white cardigans whilst he called out, "Bee!" after her. She already knew. Billy watched her sit with a small group, while the larger group seated nearby were groaning about another insect in their House.

Billy rolled up his left t-shirt sleeve and presented the top of his arm to the tall male teacher, whose one good eye opened wide and a gasp escaped between his lips before they curled into a smile.

"What do we have here?"

There was a lot of curious chatter around them as the teacher inspected Billy's arm.

"Hmm, a frog print and...a feather. Well, well, well...that is interesting." He rubbed a thumb gently over the birthmark as if checking it was real. Convinced that it was, he pronounced Billy to be in Air House. Billy's navy cardigan seemed to mean nothing to him. Focusing on the feather he pronounced, "Crow, my dear boy!"

Miss Leadbetter stopped the inspection she was doing of a girl's kneecap, dropped the book and leapt passed the two teachers between herself and the one Billy was in front of yelling, "Stop!"

"What? I'm calling it as I see it."

"He is in Water House, Mr Grasp!" The loud voices caught the attention of not only the year sevens, but also the lunch hall, which fell silent.

Mr Grasp spoke quietly but urgently, "Don't you to want him in our House? Imagine what he could be!"

"It is imagining what he could be that makes me put him in Water House." She whispered but Billy heard her, but he pretended not to so when she gave him a comforting smile, he returned the smile.

"I want him in Air House!" stated Mr Grasp.

"He is going in Water House. I am Headmistress and I've made my decision."

She gently squeezed Billy's shoulder, "Put your cardigan back on and go sit with the rest of Water House, Billy, where you belong."

Billy stared into Mr Grasp's face; having only just realised that the only bit of white he wore was a white eye-patch over his left eye. He smiled as Billy backed away into the hall. "What could have been!" Mr Grasp called after him.

"Billy!" Jacob was seated with his new Housemates.

He waved frantically at Billy. "Come! Sit with us!"

None of them had heard the soft nervous whispers of Miss Leadbetter. They may not have been quite so keen for Billy to join them if they had.

In the centre of the circular room sat remaining staff on a platform facing out towards the children. There was another cylindrical podium in the centre. The whole room was like a beautiful barn. The smell of natural wood was incredible.

Billy was taking in the surroundings when a raucous of laughter came from across the other side of the glass doors. Billy watched a plumpish boy pulling his dropped trousers up around his waist. One of the other teachers could be clearly heard, "Jeremy, I am good friends with your mother, I think I will just take her word for what sign she believes you to be rather than look at your bottom!" Another roar of laughter before a red-faced Jeremy also took himself to Air House. He sat with Malyssa, and Billy watched him mouth that he was a moth. Once again the other tables in Air filled with moaning

Once all year sevens had been surprisingly evenly distributed among the Houses, the four members of staff walked to the centre table. Miss Leadbetter went last.

Mr Grasp sat facing Air House on the platform and gave his House a half smile and a raised eyebrow of the eye he still had. The female teacher who was friends with Jeremy's mother went to sit on the platform facing Earth House. They cheered as she sat down and waved at them.

Miss Leadbetter leant into whisper in the remaining teacher's ear before he walked onto the platform. He stood in front of Billy's House. He wore bulky black boots, which Billy could see under the table, along with black trousers, a pale blue shirt with an electric blue skinny tie trapped behind a blue waistcoat; a black blazer with tails and an electric blue mohican to match his tie. The teachers here were definitely different to what Billy was used to. The male teacher raised his hand and gave a single nod. Others in Water House were cheering and whistling.

Miss Leadbetter made her way onto the platform. She walked to the centre, then seemed to lift part of the top of the cylinder, stepped inside and lowered it back into place. She seemed to stay standing. She turned and waved simultaneously at each House with both hands, before settling in front of Water House. Billy had the distinct feeling she was keeping an eye on him.

"Welcome year sevens," she said, a broad smile on her

face, "and welcome back everyone else. Most of you know the rules, so I won't bore you with them now...I know we are all hungry." She rubbed her belly and the hall filled with laughter and agreement. "Year sevens, your Heads of House will inform you of the rules before the day is through, so don't panic. You have met the Heads, as they joined me in discerning your Houses."

She signalled for the three Heads of Houses to stand. "We have Mr Grasp of Air House; Mrs Thimble of Earth House and Mr Leadbetter of Water House." She gestured for them to be seated again.

Billy liked the appearance of Mrs Thimble, who was dressed differently to Mr Grasp in his long black trench coat and Mr and Miss Leadbetter in their three-piece suits; but she was dressed equally whacky as far as Billy was concerned. She wore green and brown camouflaged combat trousers, much like Billy's own shorts; a pale green shirt with flamboyant green frilly lapels on the front, which most definitely didn't match the combats and a dark green corduroy jacket that flowed down to mid shin. She was quite a bit older than the other Heads of Houses and her brown curly hair, which hung about her shoulders, was streaked with grey, except the front, which was dyed green.

"Before we eat together please join me in singing the school anthem. Year Sevens you may just listen if you don't know it yet."

Billy looked around the hall as several children stood with various instruments, guitars, keyboards, flutes, and violins...*how did he not notice the instruments? Did he walk around with his eyes closed?*

Billy had no choice but to listen to the anthem. The music was pretty good, but the lyrics were something else:

"Here at school: The Gifted Academy,

We care about you and care about me,

There's more to school than information,

There's more to life than education,

We are blessed with gifts beyond measure,

Gifts more precious than the most bountiful treasure,

We swear to do our best in all that we do,

We are warriors through and through,

Whether in Water, Air or Earth,

We will work with all we're worth,

We will protect each and every Humanus,

Even those who want nothing to do with us,

We will follow the Artist's way,

Thankful for blessings everyday."

The hall erupted with cheers, although there were some sneers from Air House too. They didn't seem fully happy with the lyrics, but they still said them. Miss Leadbetter congratulated them all on a job well done and then pronounced the mealtime. "Those in their final year at The Gifted Academy will be bringing the food out from the kitchens to your tables for one time only," said Miss Leadbetter, "Do not be concerned...they did not cook it." She gave a little chuckle and a wink.

The last years brought the food out. It smelt delicious. Billy hadn't smelled anything this good since he was very young, before his father died.

Despite the heat from breathing and steam from lunch, Billy was continually shivering.

Miss Leadbetter leant forward and tapped Mr Leadbetter to get up and listen to her. After a few words were exchanged, Miss Leadbetter removed her white pinstriped blazer and handed it to Mr Leadbetter. He held it by the collar and walked down the few steps from the platform. He made his way to Billy and presented him with the blazer as the rest of the hall looked on in either awe or hatred.

"I'll collect it from you later, William Wortol." He smiled and walked back to his seat on the platform, whilst Billy hurriedly put on the blazer, which swamped his tiny stature. He felt warmer very quickly especially with everyone's gaze burning into him.

Soon, though, the room was filled with the clatter of knives and forks and everyone's eyes were on their food and not him.

Billy had filled his glass plate with chips and meat-free sausages, so much so, that even Jacob, who had a mouthful of mashed potato when he spoke, said, "Cor, Billy, you never eaten before?"

Billy laughed rather than give an honest answer of how he barely ate at home. He knew Jacob was likely joking, or at least not interested in the answer because he'd gone back to stuffing himself.

Billy looked towards Miss Leadbetter, her forearms were exposed and he clearly saw a long feather mark.

"You can see Miss Leadbetter's birthmark; the feather," said Billy.

Jacob replied, "Yeah 'course it's a feather, she turned into a giant eagle today didn't she?"

"Yeah, but that's the only teacher's sign I've seen, it was just...cool."

"OK, that reminds me, Malyssa wanted me to tell you something about feathers." He carried on chewing.

Billy had to coax the information out of him, "Jacob, what did she say to you?"

"She said, 'Did you see the eagle's tail feathers earlier?'"

"Um, maybe, why?"

"She said, 'They were white'. Don't know why she told me to tell you that."

"I do," said Billy hovering a chip in front of his mouth.

"Why?" Jacob continued to talk with his mouth full.

"Because of the white and brown feather I showed you both earlier."

"Yeah, OK, but she said it was white, not brown as well," food sprayed out of Jacob's mouth, but he didn't seem too bothered by it.

"I guess she's thinking if the body feathers are brown there's the possibility that we don't see the brown of the tail feathers because they join to the body and can't be seen."

"Oh, right, I see...could do."

Billy glanced up to her, "She could be the giant bird that scared away the crow man and other creatures from my room. It would explain why she's being so nice to me, more than the others."

An hour or so later everyone was stuffed and the tables were clear all except for drinks. Miss Leadbetter sipped from her glass and then called for attention above the noise. The hall was in stunned silence, the older children included, having forgotten how loud she could be and how much her voice carried. Jeremy choked on his drink and coughed and spluttered. Malyssa patted him on the back and handed him a tissue.

"Thank you for your attention. Firstly, I'm sure during the dinner you noticed our guardians lining the walls of the hall." Up until now they had gone unnoticed by seemingly everyone. But now as Billy's attention had been drawn to them he noticed men, women and children in outfits similar to the teachers: suits and shirts of varying colours. There were as many of them as there were students and teachers, but all on the small side. *How had he missed them?*

"They will soon become like part of the furniture as you go about your studies. Do not interact with them unless they interact with you, they are on serious missions to protect us."

Gasps bounced off the walls from the new students, but Miss Leadbetter dismissed any concerns the students had and continued with academy business.

"It is now time for our first years to receive their welcome gifts to The Gifted Academy," she cried.

"Excellent! I can't wait to wear mine!" said Jacob quietly to Billy.

"Wear what? What are we getting?"

"You'll see, I don't want to spoil it for you."

"Get in lines in front of your Head of House please, year sevens!" instructed Miss Leadbetter, "Chop chop! Quickly now!"

Billy and Jacob were in the middle of the line. However excited Jacob was he still let Billy in front of him.

"Don't look at what the others walk away with, Billy, you want it to be a surprise."

"OK, OK, Jacob. I'm not sure where to look now."

"Look at the floor, I'll tell you when to move, Mate."

Jacob did just as he said he would and safely guided Billy until he was in front of Mr Leadbetter.

"Ah, Billy, I've been told you prefer 'Billy' to 'William', apologies for before. It's nice to see you again and present you with your gifts," said Mr Leadbetter turning to reach from boxes behind him. Billy couldn't believe it, he was getting two gifts or more...one was more than enough.

He placed a leather pouch with a leather thong around Billy's neck. It had a picture embroidered on it.

"What's that?" asked Billy pointing at the embroidery, which was difficult to see properly upside down.

"That is The Gifted Academy badge," he replied, "Wear it with pride." He turned round again and produced something about the same size as the necklace pouch. "Wear this with even more pride." Mr Leadbetter handed him something cold and metal with a two-toned blue image on it.

"What is it?"

"That is a belt buckle, which you slip onto the belt that comes with your uniform." He was smiling at Billy...a lot.

"What's the blue?"

"That is Water House badge." Billy tried to take a closer look at it, but Mr Leadbetter grabbed his hand for a shake, or so Billy thought, but he didn't shake it. He instead placed his other hand on top so that Billy's hand was sandwiched between his, "Look at me," he said gently but firmly. Billy looked up into the blue eyes of Mr Leadbetter; he had crow's feet by his eyes too. "Trust her, Billy, she knows what she's doing. You're supposed to be in this House." He smiled and let Billy's hand go. "You had best go," Mr Leadbetter said, "I've held up the line with you and the boy behind you looks like he's about to burst." He chuckled.

Billy moved aside and watched as Jacob rushed forward and repeatedly thanked Mr Leadbetter before, during and after receiving his gifts. Billy quietly laughed until Jacob was told to move away now that he had received his pouch and buckle.

Jacob pulled an excited grin and held the buckle next to the pouch around his neck, "Look! Aren't they brilliant!" he said over-joyed. "Our mums will be so proud of us!"

Billy looked at the floor, "Yeah," he agreed out loud, but inside he was remembering how his mother didn't even want him to be here. Jacob frowned and looked at Billy confused, "You didn't have to give the jacket back?"

"Oh, no, he didn't ask for it," he replied, "I guess he'll get it from me later."

"Cool! Let's go sit down again and look at our gifts!"

Jacob led the way back to the glass circular table they'd been sitting at before. He took his pouch off and placed it next to the buckle on the table.

Billy followed suit. He looked closely at them. "I understand why the House one is in tones of blue, but what's on it?" Billy picked the buckle up to look closer at it.

"It's a turtle with waves on its shell in a circular pattern."

Billy squinted at the shell. He could make out three waves in a circle now they had been pointed out to him. He put it in his pocket for safe keeping until he could slip it onto his belt.

He pointed at the leather pouch connected to the leather thong necklace, "And this?"

"Oh, this has symbols for each House, see?" He pointed at the blue section, "This is Water, and you can see the three wavy lines in alternate light blue and dark blue. Then, if you look at this circle you'll see green and brown stripes, and the third circle is white with silver dots."

"OK, now I can see that. What's in the over lapping bits?"

"A mixture of the two over-lapped and in the centre is all three over-lapped."

Billy saw the three over-lapping circles and the different sections patterned with blue and green stripes; a green block with white dots; and a blue block with white dots, but in the very centre he could see blue and grccn stripes with white dots...just about.

His focus was suddenly disrupted. "Please follow the staff to your dormitories year sevens! Remember to pick up your things by the entrance!" instructed Miss Leadbetter. "The rest of you are dismissed for the day to get reacquainted with the grounds. Remember: using your keys here without permission is strictly prohibited and punishable." She gave them all another wink and stepped down from the podium, whilst the older students ran from the hall. She didn't seem at all bothered by their charging about. *She had a funny sense of humour,* thought Billy, *how could they use a key that was just a metaphor for being a part of The Gifted Academy? There was nothing to open! It must be some joke they're all in on, although nobody else is laughing.*

Billy made his way to the entrance. Jacob helped him get his rucksack back on his back and Billy returned the favour. He was about to start walking with the other year sevens in his House when he was tapped on the head.

"Billy, may I walk and talk with you?"

"Of course, Mr Leadbetter," he replied confused.

"Very gracious of you, thank you." Mr Leadbetter moved to Billy's left where he wasn't being hit with the large glass bowl. He glanced at Jacob, who quickly got the hint and ran to catch up with a group in front of them.

"You want the jacket now?" asked Billy.

"No, wait until we reach the cabin."

Thank goodness! Billy was relieved he didn't have to take his luggage off and put it back on again.

"I want to explain more about why I'm pleased you're in my House, when I'm aware you have two birthmarks like The Beast. I believe that if Miss Leadbetter says something, it's usually right."

"How can you be so sure?"

"The evidence I've witnessed over my life and I've known her my whole life, after all, she is my twin sister." He smiled at Billy.

"That explains the same last name and similar appearance."

"Yes, quite, although most people who were in Water House dress like this...to some degree."

"OK." Billy wanted to refocus Mr Leadbetter, "What evidence have you seen?"

"More than I can share with you right now. She has gifts and talents that people could not even imagine. And although she's not perfect, just as no-one is, she has a very good heart, which seems to guide her in good decisions, in the way of the Artist, most of the time."

"You're convinced that I should be in Water House,

like Miss Leadbetter said?"

"Yes, of course. The Houses are named not just by the birthmarks and gifts its members possess, but are linked also with the three elements of the person: mind, body and soul. Air House represents those that use their minds primarily; Earth House use their bodies and Water obviously use their souls."

"It still doesn't explain why I should be in Water." Billy kicked up some leaves as they walked, all the new information was overwhelming him and frustrating.

"Billy, what is soul? Nobody really knows do they? It's a mystery that somehow connects us with the Artist, creator of all. People don't understand why you have two birthmarks and therefore gifts, which makes you a mystery." He ruffled Billy's blonde curls, "If that doesn't qualify you to be in Water House, I don't know what will!" He laughed a kind laugh.

"They say The Beast had the same two over-lapping birthmarks, was he in this House too?"

"Ah, no, he was in Air House."

"Well, that's something good then, isn't it?" said Billy smiling.

"Well, yes, I guess it is."

"Mr Leadbetter, can I ask you some questions about

him, you know, The Beast?"

"Yes, I will see what I can answer for you."

Billy took a deep breath working out which question to start with.

"Oh, I know, I'll start with this: what was it he did that was so evil, that everyone is so scared about him plotting and hiding?"

Mr Leadbetter rubbed the beard on his chin, which was ginger not electric blue like his hair. "OK, I don't think it's appropriate for you to know everything as a first year. But, basically, he turned on us all and attacked and killed many who got in his way to the top. We've held him off over the centuries, as best we can, no matter who he has been, but he's out there somewhere."

"But why did he do it?"

"Power, Billy. He seeks power and adulation equal to the Artist. He believed himself to be something special, a chosen one, because of his two birthmarks, and being part Guardian. He believes he's picked to reign supreme over us all including those in the other realm, who we are called to protect not reign over."

Billy sighed and thought about his next question, "Where is he?"

"No-one knows. He could be hiding anywhere in this

realm or the other, although I doubt he would be in the other realm for too long, when his followers are here and he can do more here. Plus, this realm is a lot bigger than just The Gifted Academy."

Billy hadn't thought about there being more than what he was seeing.

Mr Leadbetter continued to explain, "If this was all there was in this realm, Billy, there wouldn't be much to conquer and rule now, would there?"

Billy thought hard and kicked some more leaves, "I guess not."

"He'd be ruling the world you've been living in for so long if there weren't so many of us. The Beast could have gone straight for the ungifted Humanums, that's what we call them, if it wasn't for the gifted protecting them - after all, why should we have these gifts and be chosen for no other reason than to love and help, surely?"

Billy stayed silent. It was a lot for an eleven-year-old brain to process, even for someone as clever as he was.

"Those of us who have been taught or work at The Gifted Academy particularly like its name above others. Shall I tell you why, Billy?"

"Yes, please," he replied, knowing that Mr Leadbetter was on a roll and would probably tell him anyway. He didn't mind getting answers to questions he didn't even ask...it saved him asking them another time.

"Strictly speaking, its name derives from the fact that we have special gifts coming through our bloodlines, which is what The Beast and his followers focussed on. But those of us who are against him think of us being the gift to the ungifted, as their protectors, even those that choose to have nothing to do with the Artist. A gift is free. We fight a war they don't even know is being fought or needs to be fought."

Billy thought back over his eleven years of not knowing about the war being fought. Somewhere in the back of his mind he thought he knew more than his mind was revealing to him, like he already had first hand knowledge and experience of the battle. He shuddered. "What would happen if The Beast were ruler?"

"Ah! That doesn't even bear to be thought about, let alone voiced at this time. But, terrible things would happen. More terrible than you have ever known." Mr Leadbetter shook his thoughts away.

"Look! We're here!"

Billy had been so busy listening and forming pictures in his mind he hadn't noticed his surroundings.

Chapter Six

Tree Houses

The sight before Billy was phenomenal: a spectacle so tall that standing directly in front of it, he couldn't see the top.

"This is our dormitory?" Billy asked, his eyes nearly popping out of his head.

"Sure is!" replied Mr Leadbetter, "I'd get going if I were you, it's first come; first served here."

As Billy looked around he saw lots of the older kids had come to view the year sevens claim their spaces. He overheard one boy exclaim with joy, "This is going to be interesting, wonder who is going to get stuck at the top in the camp bed since there's an extra one of them."

Another boy with muscles as big as tree trunks said, "Survival of the fittest lads!" They fell about laughing.

Billy still hadn't moved one step closer to the multi-storey tree House before him. It's cylindrical shape made of wood wrapped around several tall trees towered above him. Immediately in front was a large log cabin, which was the ground floor. Then there were four smaller round log cabins working their way into the treetops to the left and four to the right. The storeys were linked together by spiral staircases on the left and right. He noticed some wood and rope bridges leading to large cylindrical crows' nests, like on ships; not the birds. There was rigging hanging from them to the ground too.

"Billy! Up here! Hurry!" Billy looked up to see Jacob's smiling face sticking out of an open window in the highest cabin. The top storey was smaller than the others, but just as tall. It looked pointier where it was much narrower.

Billy loved the whole thing; even the roof tiles were wooden.

"Come on, Billy! I can only save you the bed next to mine for so long! Simon and James are on their way up!"

Billy started running towards the left hand staircase, but one of the large boys, the one with all the muscles, called out to him, "Take the inside staircase, Kid!" Billy hadn't noticed there was a staircase going straight up between the left and right dormitories and joined to the cabins by rope and wooden footbridges.

"Thanks!" Billy ran inside the cabin winding his way along small wooden spiral steps. He whipped open the glass doors and stepped inside. Inside was possibly even more breath-taking than the outside! A narrow wooden staircase spiralled its way through to the top of the cabin. The wood grain was beautiful, with a yellow tinge and not faded by weather like the outside.

Billy didn't have time to take everything in, he had to race to the top. As he twisted up towards the highest point, the smell of sawdust filled his senses. He inhaled deeply filling his lungs with the natural wood scent.

The stairs were so solid they didn't creak. All he could hear was the thud of his footsteps upon the rigid wood. As he climbed the staircase he got dizzier and slower. At some points he held out an arm to the banister to support himself as he caught his breath, or at least tried to. He was thankful for the staircase being in the outdoors between each storey. He climbed past four storeys; the next was his final destination.

He wound his way through the final steps and into the

final crows nest. Placing one foot in front of the other, he stepped across the wooden bridge, which wavered slightly from side to side as his weight shifted. Ten steps further. He burst through a glass door into his dormitory making such a noise he grabbed Jacob's attention.

"There you are, Mate! Good idea to come through the centre! Big traffic jam on the outside!" Jacob ran to Billy's side and helped him remove his luggage from his back.

"Am-I-last?" Billy asked between deep breaths.

"No, Mate! Bobby and Sean beat you, and Simon and James decided to go over there." Billy followed the directions Jacob pointed in from Bobby, a tall boy with red hair cut short, to Sean an equally tall boy with dark brown hair in a sort of crop with a flick at the front and finally to Simon and James, who basically looked like a slightly smaller version of Jacob. "They're my cousins...on my mum's side."

Jacob kindly unrolled Billy's sleeping bag onto the bed next to his, and leant his rucksack against the bed so that Billy could take his time to arrange his items on the pine bedside cabinet and the wooden ottoman at the foot of the bed.

The sleeping bag had the House emblem on. So did the curtains, which were also blue but with the House

Badge repeated all over them. Every bed had a window that was framed by the curtains. Billy suddenly remembered the older boy's words.

"There's twelve beds and thirteen boys in our year, where does unlucky number thirteen sleep?"

"Look up, Mate," replied Jacob.

A rope ladder hung in the middle of the room and there was a platform covering half the tower. "What's up there?"

"Have a look...we did. Looks like Lesley's going to be last, and a while yet."

Billy climbed the rope ladder, which was sturdier than he expected, before he realised it was fastened to the floor. The ladder went to the top of the tower not just to the platform, which had a wooden rail all round it. Jacob followed him up. There were some simple wooden cabinets and a camp bed set up in the middle below a small window wit a single curtain over it.

"This space is usually used as extra storage for the House, but they've had to turn it into an extra sleeping area. First time ever!"

"Still, pretty nice considering it's only a camp bed. Maybe we could take it in turns to sleep up here?" suggested Billy.

Jacob screwed up his face, "Maybe *you* could, but *I* got up here first, *I* deserve a real bed to sleep in."

"I can ask the others."

"They aren't going to do it either. You're on your own with this idea, Mate." Jacob slapped him on the shoulder. "Come on, let's go back down and get unpacked properly. Then we can check out the lounge downstairs. Did you see the size of it!"

Half hour later Billy and Jacob were unpacked. They waited for Simon and James before proceeding down the central staircase that Billy had made his way up earlier. It was a lot easier going down, especially without luggage.

They reached the bottom quickly without the extra weight.

"Wow! Look at this place!" said James, "I thought our dorms were cool, but this is something else!"

"Yeah! Look at the log fire over there!" cried Simon.

Billy couldn't help but notice how Simon and James also sounded very similar to Jacob. *Must be nice to have a big family,* he thought.

There were several wooden tables and chairs scattered around the cabin and some leather couches and armchairs with blue blankets and throws on them. The couches sat around a thick blue rug in front of the log fire. Some of the other boys already occupied the tables and couches. The muscular boy was seated on the couch and turned to Billy when he heard the young voices, not yet broken, nearby. "Kid, did you make it?"

"Yes, thanks," replied Billy, who could feel his friends gawping at him and turning his face red.

Billy moved away to the other side of the room and sat on a little wooden rocking chair facing outside. Jacob plonked himself in the one next to him, "You know that Sixth Form boy?"

"No," replied Billy.

"But, he's talking to you like you do." Jacob seemed in awe of Billy.

"He gave me the advice of taking the centre staircase earlier. I don't know why...but I'm grateful."

"That's so cool!"

"OK." Billy wasn't sure why it was 'so cool' for a Sixth Form boy to speak to him; he wasn't even used to kids his own age speaking to him. He couldn't work out the difference yet.

Mr Leadbetter appeared at the doorway to the lounge.

"Year Sevens, gather round please."

As all the first years gathered it was the first time that

Billy realised there were girls in the lounge. He'd completely overlooked the fact that it was a shared lounge. Not that it was a problem, just a bit of a shock.

"OK, is that everyone?"

Everyone nodded.

"Great! Ordinarily you have your meals in the Round Hall like at lunch, but we like to give the first years a campfire on the first night. So, please, boys and girls, go collect firewood. The forest is full of it, and bring it to the fire pit, which is a little way further along the path you took to get here."

All 25 first years took to the woodlands. Billy set off with Jacob in tow.

"Billy, where are you rushing to? There are trees everywhere," said Jacob.

"Those are beech trees over there. The wood from those will be great. It's slow burning. Pick up as many dead twigs and branches as possible." He bent down as soon as he reached the beech trees, gathering as much as he could.

"How do you know this?" asked Jacob.

"I read a lot about nature. Like I read that we have to be careful of the knots in the fire because they will spit." Billy hesitated before he continued with his answer,

"Plus, we, um, sometimes had to make fires in the garden at home."

"Oh, why?"

Billy didn't answer straightaway. He felt embarrassed. It was getting awkward, so eventually he answered, "Mum couldn't always pay the bills so we wouldn't have gas and electricity." Billy flushed red. But Jacob didn't even falter before responding, "No shame in that, Mate. It happens, trust me, I know."

Billy stopped picking up sticks and looked hopefully at Jacob, "It happened to you?"

"Yeah, Mate, all the time!"

Billy exhaled relieved. "But you didn't know about firewood?"

"Well, no. We're a big family, so I didn't have to. That, and I was never trusted with stuff like that."

Billy laughed at his wonderful friend, who joined in the laughter. They ran to the fire pit multiple times. It looked like a proper campfire, like those that Billy had only ever seen in books; with large logs around it to sit on. A lot of the kids were already there and a fire was blazing in the centre. It looked amazing and night was only just drawing in on their last visit.

"What are we eating?" called Daniel, "I'm starving!"

"Well, you've got to wait Master Daniel," said Mr Leadbetter. "Ms Humour has put on some baked potatoes, apples filled with sugar, and bananas with chocolate buttons. Oh, and various vegetables including meat-free sausages like you had at lunch."

Billy spent the evening chatting with his new friends and singing songs around the campfire. Before long Billy watched as the flames slowly flickered and died and the embers glowed softly red in the ash of the pit. The stars twinkled overhead. He stifled a yawn. He needn't have bothered hiding it, everybody was yawning.

Ms Humour turned to Mr Leadbetter, "I think it's high time these youngsters got to bed, don't you think?"

"Yes, quite, quite." Mr Leadbetter's way of talking didn't seem to match his exterior, thought Billy. This thought was his last conscious act before he along, with others walked like sleep walkers to their dormitories and to bed.

The next conscious thought Billy had was when he awoke the following morning, snug as a bug in a rug in his sleeping bag. When he stirred properly and sat up and looked around, to his horror the beds were empty and so was the room. In fact, he couldn't hear any voices. He looked at his watch, 8:20. "Oh no! I'm going to miss breakfast!" He rushed to get dressed into his new school uniform. The same navy cardigan from the day before over a pale blue shirt, black trousers and black boots. The look was completed with a two-tone wavy-lined blue tie. Putting the tie on was a new experience. An experience he hoped would get easier as he repeated it! Ties were uncomfortable even if it didn't look like it.

He bolted to the Round Hall for breakfast but everyone was leaving to get to class. His stomach rumbled. *What a great way to start the first official day!*

He turned to follow his classmates.

"Billy! You missed breakfast!" Jacob called after him having come from the hall last. "I waited 'till last, but you didn't show."

"I know; I woke up late."

"I saved you this." Jacob held out a sausage sandwich. "It's meat-free sausage with a bit of ketchup," he laughed, "You seem to like those."

Billy smiled and accepted the sandwich. He ravaged it quickly whilst walking to class, making sure not to drip ketchup on his clothes. "Everything's vegetarian here?"

"Yeah, did you eat meat at home?" Jacob looked disgusted at the thought.

"Well, no," replied Billy, "But I just thought that we

couldn't afford it."

"No, it's not that. We manifest or turn into animals, and although we're not real animals, still eating something that looks like your manifested friend is slightly cannibalistic!"

They, along with a mixture of other kids from the three Houses, spilled into the room for their first lesson. Not an unusual one, just maths.

A woman dressed in a black satin dress and a white rose in a buttonhole turned round from the white board to face the class with pen in hand. Jacob was horrified that they were sitting at the front until he looked up at the teacher facing them. Her long wavy white hair hung loosely below her shoulders, shaping her dark brown face.

"Close your mouth, Jacob," whispered Billy, sniggering.

"I'm Miss Shuttle and I will be teaching you maths." Her voice was as beautiful as honey.

Malyssa and Jeremy had joined the row with Billy and Jacob.

"Much like in the Humanum realm, we need maths to buy and sell items and ours works the same as the metric system fortunately, although I would like to point out that we had the system first. So, you can whine at having to study maths, but think how fortunate you are that it matches the realm you come from. Think of the other countries' academies where the other realms money doesn't use the metric system. Yes, you are fortunate!"

A voice mumbled behind Billy, "Doesn't feel very fortunate. Got to be a waste of a class to be taught by the likes of her!" He nodded his head in Miss Shuttle's direction. His friends nearby laughed.

"Something you would like to share, Jake?"

Jake scoffed. Billy turned to look at him. Jake wasn't much taller than him and he had curly hair like him too. But Jake's was pitch black, matching his eyes. His complexion was so pale and he wore a long black trench coat over his white cardigan. He looked more like a vampire than a boy. Billy expected his manifested animal to be a bat.

Before Jeremy could stop her, Malyssa repeated everything that Jake had said.

"Is that so? Please see me at break, Jake," said Miss Shuttle smoothly.

Jake scowled at Malyssa and mouthed, "You'll pay for that, *Bug*!"

"I want to find out where we need to work from, so

115

today will be a thorough test covering what you should know already."

A groan escaped the lips of every student except Billy, who smiled at the prospect of something he was good at. He flew through the paper despite the paper balls being thrown into his hair by Jake and his cronies, who were jealous that he finished with fifteen minutes to spare. Whilst Miss Shuttle was occupied ticking his paper, he sat with his back to the fire of paper balls.

Eventually, the class finished and they all shuffled out of the room.

'Billy, are you going to be teacher's pet? Want Shuttle to throw you a treat?" Jake mocked as they left him. His buddies Lewis and Jennifer laughed.

"Stop it, Jake!" ordered Malyssa.

"Stop it, Jake!" mimicked Jake in a high-pitched voice. "Don't talk to me, Bug! You're as bad as her in there!"

"You can't talk about Miss Shuttle like that, she's a teacher," said Malyssa.

"Yeah, of a pointless other realm subject. I don't need to know maths, my parents are so rich we don't ask the cost of stuff, we just get the servant to hand over our stones." He smiled smugly.

"You might not have it all one day," said Malyssa.

"You haven't even got it now, if you did, you'd be wearing new uniform...without holes. I saw you having to shop at the second hand stalls. What a loser!"

Billy hadn't noticed the holes in Malyssa's clothing before Jake pointed them out. He'd gone to school for years with clothing the same way, he didn't think anything of it.

"Malyssa, come on, he's not worth it." Billy tugged on her arm.

"Worth more than you, Water Boy, and that guppy next to you!"

Jacob got mad, and Simon and James had to hold him back from attacking Jake.

Malyssa walked away with Billy and the other boys.

"Yep, go off with your boyfriend!" Jake called after Malyssa. "Told you they shouldn't put you lot with the rest of us Air types! You're a mockery to the Air House!"

Jake started walking after them, still calling out cruel remarks. "You too, Jeremy. You're a bug! They should make a fourth House for you insects, so you can be kept away from the rest of us."

Lewis and Jennifer said nothing, but laughed. They probably didn't even understand Jake.

"Better yet," continued Jake, an extra flare of menace

in his tone, "They should just squash you at birth!"

Billy took a sideways glance at Malyssa. He watched a tear roll down her cheek. He stayed silent. He wasn't going to give that brute the satisfaction of knowing he'd made Malyssa cry. Bullies didn't deserve the satisfaction. He, Jacob, Jeremy and Malyssa stood at the front of the next class so that the other kids didn't see Malyssa's tear streaked face.

PART TWO
THE LEARNING

Chapter Seven
Lessons in Manifesting

The next lesson was outside. The class made their way to a small lake. The water was still and green. No life could be seen in the lake except for some spindly-legged pond skaters skittering across the lake's surface.

A long, rickety wooden dock led out towards the centre of the lake. Large grey rocks were scattered at intervals around the lake, like huge stepping-stones, except you'd have to be a giant to step from one to the other. Billy could hear insects buzzing near by in the reeds around the water's edge. He enjoyed the peaty smell of algae in the fresh air. The scent soothed his soul after recent events. Malyssa, too, had stopped crying and her face was drying in the cool air.

Overhead a fast birdcall chattered ruining the silence. A magpie swooped towards them, its unmistakable black and white plumage and iridescent green-blue glossy sheen caught in the sunlight. It landed in front of the children and cawed before growing and morphing into a human. Before them, stood the tall and scary form of Mr Grasp. The white eye-patch over his left eye and his long black coat, that shimmered in the sunlight like his feathers had. He fixed his one good eye on Billy and smiled before scanning the rest of the children.

"That is how you manifest from animal to human flawlessly!" he bellowed, spittle flying from his mouth. "You will be manifesting from human to animal!"

The class exchanged eager glances, until Mr Grasp's next statement, "I'm not going to give you the steps to change, but give a scenario where you will have to change or face the unpleasant consequences."

Jake's friends patted him on the back, which Mr Grasp clocked. "Ah, yes, Jake, your mother told me you have already done this and are a natural. But, from my understanding we have one among us who has semi-manifested; a much harder fete." He glared at Billy, "But, I don't believe it to be his true animal, because he has another...isn't that right, Billy?"

The class gasped except Jacob and Malyssa, who already knew of his two birthmarks. The rhetoric was lost on Billy and he responded, "I have not shown any evidence of two animals except for the mark."

Mr Grasp winked at him like they were friends, "But, you will, Billy. You were meant for better things than the Water House can give you and I am determined to nurture that within you."

"Miss Leadbetter is adamant I'm in Water House," he replied firmly.

"We shall see, won't we?" He returned to talking to the entire class. "Let's have you in pairs..." The children began to move towards friends, "Of my choosing!" hollered Mr Grasp followed by the groans of the class.

"Blossom and Jeremy, Malyssa and Simon, Jacob and Daniel..." he continued through the list of names until only two were left and both were equally disappointed with the outcome, "Billy and Jake!" Mr Grasp smirked at his ingenious idea. It was only in the pairing up that Billy realised the extra student was not in their classes.

"Sir! This is outrageous! You can't pair me up with him!" Jake screamed at Mr Grasp, who didn't bat an eyelid, "Wait till I tell my mother! She - "

Mr Grasp cut Jake off, "- I will tell your darling mother the same as I will tell you now: William Wortol, aka, Billy, has the potential to be of great credit to the Air House when he is rightfully placed there. Until then I will call out the winged creature in him by any and every means and I want to use the best ways possible and in this class, that is you Jake Fester."

The compliment tickled Jake's ego and mellowed him.

"Let's make this more interesting." Mr Grasp rubbed his bald head whilst thinking. The grimace that spread across his face told the onlookers when his plan had formed.

"Each pair will be marked out of twenty; that's ten points each for your manifestations. You need to focus your minds for this. If you are in Air House, this should come naturally...for most of you." He looked begrudgingly at Jeremy and Malyssa. Malyssa felt her face flush with anger, but Jeremy placed a sly, gentle hand on her arm, to ease her frustration and warn her. Mr Grasp grinned at them both. It made Billy sick to see a teacher so openly talk so negatively about students.

Mr Grasp continued with his lesson, "You are to run as fast as you can along the dock and manifest before the end of the dock, or you shall plummet into the lake as a fully clothed person. And none of us want that do we, Blossom?" He sniggered, and Jake and his posse sniggered too.

"Jake! Why don't you demonstrate how to do it!"

Jake took up position at the beginning of the dock. He was bent towards the ground like many an Olympic sprinter.

"Go!" yelled Mr Grasp.

Jake took off full pelt towards the lake. The wooden planks bounced with every footfall. He was fast, much faster than Billy. He reached the end of the dock and launched himself into the air where he transformed into a small bat, flitting through the sky and back to the class where he morphed back to his human form before landing.

The Air House members, including Mr Grasp cheered and whistled. Even Billy had to admit he was impressed; but also a little amused that Jake did indeed turn into a bat like he'd predicted the vampire boy would.

"Excellent, Jake!" Mr Grasp gave him a friendly smack on the back. Nine out of ten! Just need to be a little smoother changing back."

Jake applauded himself.

"OK, the rest of the pairs, label yourselves one and

two. All number ones form a line at the beginning of the dock."

Blossom had somehow ended up next. She shook with fear. She began to run, but was slow. She was plumper than Jake, not fat, just a little stocky. She thudded along the deck. As she reached the end she leapt into the air and...came back down ending in the water, fully clothed with a huge splash. Air House fell about laughing, well those like Jake did; others looked with dread to their own turn. Most children followed suit.

"Here's a tip for those of you who are less agile animals of the earth and will not reach the rock even if you do morph: change before you reach the edge and give yourself room to stop before falling off the edge." He chuckled cruelly at the foolish wet children dripping by the water's edge.

"Number twos, step up!" He shouted, "Billy, you first! Don't let me down! Let me see your winged creature. Think about how much better a bird would be, to match that feather mark you have, rather than a tiny frog!"

Malyssa piped up, "Billy, remember, Miss Leadbetter knows what she's doing, she's the Headmistress. She believes you're in the right House already."

Billy nodded.

Mr Grasp shot Malyssa daggers, "Even Headmistresses make mistakes! You noticed I didn't mention any *bugs* in my list of excellent winged-creatures? Remember that! Bugs are always slow to learn and a disgrace to the Air House."

Billy couldn't believe what he was hearing. School in the other realm may not have been pleasant with the other children, but teachers would never act this way. In fact, he always got on better with teachers because they were pleasant.

Malyssa had had quite enough of the insults for one morning, she sprinted along the dock and threw herself off the end and buzzed into the air in her animal form. She flew back as a bumblebee buzzing a few times around Jake before manifesting back into her human form. The children from Earth and Water Houses, plus Jeremy, cheered with admiration.

Mr Grasp furrowed his eyebrows and clenched his jaw, "Five out of ten for going without being asked to!"

Malyssa didn't care, she'd done better than most of her House, who were birds, and not even Mr Grasp could take away this moment of joy for her as she looked at the jealous faces. She faced Billy saying, "Be true to yourself. You don't need to do something just to win...it may not be the win you want!"

Billy thought Malyssa was proving to be mentally a lot older than her eleven years. He liked it, he felt an odd connection to her by the way she thought. Was it an Air House thing?

"Billy, just go!" order Mr Grasp.

"Don't let me down!" shouted Jake.

He stepped up to the dock, closed his eyes and breathed deeply. Quickly, he ran to the end and leapt into the air as others had, and down, down, down he tumbled and plopped into the lake with barely a splash. He disappeared beneath the surface.

The children watched from the edge of the lake. Billy stayed beneath the water.

His legs kicked with strength against the water and caught in his webbed feet propelling him through twists and turns in the water. He suddenly hopped from the water to a rock in the lake nearest the dock. He could barely be seen by the children at only two centimetres in length. He sat upon the rock, waiting for someone to notice.

Blossom suddenly called out, "Hey! He's there...I think!"

They squinted at the forest green frog with black and

brown blotches. Billy dived into the water disappearing beneath the surface once again. He did not want to resurface anytime soon. In the cool of the lake he felt completely free.

He pushed the water away from himself with all four legs moving gracefully through the water. It was a lot clearer within the water than looking from above. Before long, Billy realised the lake wasn't as lifeless as he had first thought. He noticed minnows darting between rocks and weeds. Usually they were small, but compared to him now, they were huge.

Above the surface, back on dry land, there was quite a commotion. Mr Leadbetter had been watching from nearby but out of sight. He knew what Mr Grasp's first lesson of the year was like, and was himself curious as to how Billy would get on with his first challenge. He had shown himself not too long after he expected Billy to reappear out of the water.

"Where is he?"

Mr Grasp shrugged and said, "Somewhere in there. He hasn't come out. Foolish boy was showing off and hasn't returned."

"He is not foolish!" Mr Leadbetter glared at Mr Grasp. "Please tell me you told them what's in there before you challenged them!"

"Well...not exactly," said Mr Grasp.

"Not at all!" exclaimed Malyssa. "What is in there?"

"Carp!"

"Carp! Oh no! You've got to do something!"

"I'll do something!" yelled Jacob, readying himself for his run-up along the deck.

"No, you're a fish, not much bigger than he is as a frog, all you'll do is give the carp an appetiser."

Jacob gulped pleased he'd announced his action and was stopped before he carried them out. "He was going to let us all land in the water when there's carp and other things that could attack and eat us in there?"

Mr Leadbetter surprisingly came to Mr Grasp's defence, "He is a qualified teacher at the academy, and there's nothing wrong with being a small animal in the lake when you know the dangers to expect. You can watch out for them and be out as soon as possible, but Billy doesn't know what's in there and will more than likely be having a jolly old unsuspecting swim!"

"So, what do we do now?" asked Malyssa with urgency, "We can't let him get eaten!"

"I'll go in!" Mr Leadbetter ran along the dock and dived into the water. He manifested before brcaking through the surface.

The children looked on in awe of the magnificent but terrifying creature as it splashed into the lake. They watched the giant grey body disappear, until all that was seen was the triangular fin of the Great White Shark. If the carp didn't terrify Billy, the shark would.

Mr Leadbetter tore through the body of water, searching out for the tiny shape of Billy. In a matter of seconds he saw Billy, swimming carefree away from the shore. Following Billy was a half metre in length carp. It glided smoothly behind Billy.

Just as the carp was speeding up to make his move Mr Leadbetter launched himself through the carp, knocking it out of the way and capturing Billy in his mouth. The spectators saw the ripples of water on the surface. They watched Mr Leadbetter's fin approach the water's edge until he appeared as a human, knee deep in the water with Billy in his arms.

Billy was limp. Mr Leadbetter laid him on the grass. The class ran over to them.

"Stay back!" He swallowed water and he's not breathing! He drank it in when I caught him in shock." Mr Leadbetter performed CPR, breathing air into Billy's lungs until Billy coughed and spluttered. He sat up and coughed some more. Lake water trickled down his chin and caused dark patches on his blue shirt.

"Sh-shark!" He yelled shaking and pointing at the lake.

"Calm down, Billy," said Mr Leadbetter, "That was me. Do you think you can stand?" He helped Billy to his feet. As soon as he let go, Malyssa launched herself at Billy embracing him in a loving hug. "Thank goodness, you're OK."

"Thank goodness!" mimicked Jake in a high-pitched voice.

"Jacob can you take Billy back to the dormitory and sit with him just to make sure he's OK, please?"

"I can do it, Mr Leadbetter," declared Malyssa.

"I'm afraid you can't, Malyssa, you are not allowed in the Water House cabins. But, thank you for your kind offer. I'm sure Billy appreciates your kindness." He smiled warmly at her.

Jacob moved towards Billy, "Come on Mate, let's get you back."

They walked in silence back to the cabin, winding the steps to the lounge. They plonked themselves on the brown couches draped in blue throws.

"You doing OK, Mate?" asked Jacob.

"This place is weird."

Jacob got up and started the log fire with the matches on the mantle.

"Yeah, I guess so. Maybe that's why some people turn down coming here."

"What happens if they change their mind later in life? I mean, it's weird, but I don't want to leave."

"You only get one chance to go to an academy like this as a child, so if you refuse in the first year and change your mind, you forfeit the gift. The Artist doesn't give up on you though and you can choose later in life and go to an Adult Academy, but they're not nearly as fun!"

Billy was grateful that Jacob was being normal with him, not making a great fuss over his well-being. He was curious about Jacob's family, they never got further in discussing things after the campfire.

"Jacob, Simon and James are your cousins, right?"

"Right."

"And you said you have an older sister here?"

"Yeah, she's in her fourth year, Year Ten."

"Who else is there?"

Jacob thought for a second trying to picture his family tree, "Well, I've got an older brother, but he works now he's finished here. He lives over with my cousins in Africa, still in this realm though. He's an elephant, so he's got loads of strength and uses it to do heavy lifting jobs out there. Met a girl in his fifth year on an exchange here and followed her out there as soon as he could."

"OK," said Billy puzzled.

"Mate, I don't know why he travelled that far for a girl either, but he just said I'd understand when I'm older and fall in love." He pulled a disgusted face, "I don't want to fall in love, girls are nice and all but I don't want to be tied down." He leant back on the couch and slumped.

"What do you mean?" asked Billy.

"Don't know, Mate, just something one of my cousins said." He started laughing and Billy joined in.

Billy looked out of the window. The sky was grey. Raindrops tapped on the window and wooden cabin. The pitter-patter of rain mixed with the crackle of the fire was music to Billy's ears and brought a sense of peace.

Billy closed his eyes and focussed on his other senses. His mind stilled and he drifted off to sleep.

Screaming filled the lounge and he sat bolt up.

"What? What is it?" Jacob woke up to the screaming too.

Billy ruffled his own hair in a self-soothing way.

"Crow man found me here. But, but...I wasn't me." Billy was sweating; his skin was pale.

"What do you mean?"

"I-I was a bird standing before Crow man. Well, I wasn't all bird, I'd semi-manifested into the half human and half bird creature." He shuddered.

"What bird?" Jacob sat on the edge of the couch leaning towards Billy, listening intently.

"I don't know." He rubbed his face with his hands.

"Is that all, Mate? Why did you scream?"

"He was screaming lies at me and the birds around him and some other animals started to close in on me. I couldn't escape." He ran his hands through his hair again and gripped the curls.

"Mate, calm down. It was just a dream." He patted Billy on the shoulder trying to sooth him. The colour was still drained from his face. "What was he saying to you, Mate?"

Billy hesitated before answering, "I-I don't remember now," he lied. He looked down at his feet and then up at the fire. He stared at the flickering red, orange and yellow flames as they danced seemingly to the patters of raindrops on the roof. They had their own rhythm.

A few moments later the cabin was bustling with his classmates asking him if he was OK. The events of his morning had travelled far and older boys were checking on him too. Muscle boy, whose name turned out to be Bradley, but everyone called him 'Brad', took a special interest in Billy's condition, "You sure you're OK? Can we get you anything?"

"I'm fine, thanks," replied Billy...repeatedly.

"That Grasp! He's a piece of work! Terrorises the first years every year!"

"He wasn't trying to terrorise me," stated Billy, surprised by his own defence of Mr Grasp.

"'Course he was! Does it all the time!"

"He really wasn't! Actually, he wants me to be in his House."

"You can't, you're a frog, and you're in Water House."

"But I also have a feather mark." The room fell silent. Clearly not the whole story had spread.

Chapter Eight

Bows and Arrows

"Don't worry, Mate. They were bound to find out about your two birthmarks at some point. It's over and done with now," said Jacob as they walked towards the next class led by Mrs Trumpet. He picked up a stone and lobbed it into the distant patch of trees.

"Good throw," said Billy, in an attempt to change the subject even though he knew Jacob meant well. He couldn't work out yet whether this was a good first day or a bad one. On the one hand he'd nearly died and the academy would be nervous around him now that they knew about his marks; but on the other hand, his friends had really come through for him and it was definitely great having friends. Maybe the rest of the day would help him decide one way or the other.

Jacob threw another stone aiming for a dark patch of leaves on a tree, "Getting some target practice in before our first archery lesson." He laughed at his own joke. The stone rustled and thudded as it flew and landed.

"Did you hear that?" asked Billy, suddenly anxious.

"Yeah, sounded like it carried on another few metres past those leaves I aimed at! Good, eh?" Jacob bent to pick another stone from the gravel pathway.

"No, it wasn't the stone. It sounded like a 'caw', like a bird..."

"I don't hear it."

"...Like a crow."

"Maybe you needed to rest more, Mate. I can't hear any crows. There's some birds tweeting, but I don't hear any 'caws'." Said Jacob straining to listen carefully, "And even if there were crows, they're just birds."

"But, what about Crow man...The Beast? What if it's him?"

"Then Miss Leadbetter and the other teachers would know about it." Jacob fiddled with the stone he'd picked up, rolling it around his fingers. "You're hyped up from your bad dream. It's the safest place to be."

138

"It's an academy, like a school. It's full of kids and teachers, what makes this place so safe?"

"You don't know?" Jacob raised his eyebrows.

"Know what? I told you, all this is completely new to me."

"These aren't ordinary teachers like we're used to, Billy, look at them for one. Imagine our teachers rocking up to school in those clothes, with blue or green hair and covered in piercings and tattoos? They'd never get a job in the other world as teachers!"

"So what? The rules are different here." He tilted his head to the side and pursed his lips.

"You can only be teachers in this realm if you are the best in your field. That means we are very well protected here. And...imagine what it takes to be Head!"

Billy thought about it for a moment and then smiled and nodded, satisfied by Jacob's logic.

"Come on, you don't want to be late for Mrs Trumpet, she'll pin you to a target board by your own arrows." Jacob started to jog slowly.

"Speaking of arrows," Billy's were rattling in their quiver over his shoulder, "Where are yours?"

"Um...I don't have any." Jacob cleared his throat.

"Oh, what do you have?" Billy asked, not picking up

on the awkwardness and discomfort of Jacob.

"Daggers are the cheapest weapon, so in my family we all have daggers." Jacob was downcast and he slowed back to a walk.

"You guys must be very brave!" Billy stated to Jacob's utter surprise.

"Brave? What? Why?"

"Well, daggers are short, like small swords, so in a battle you have to be up close and personal with a combatant; not like me who can stand well away and shoot arrows."

"Yeah, that's right! We are brave! That's why we have them really. Forget the 'cheap' thing I said before."

"That's why your aim when throwing is so good, too, like before with the leaves and the stones. You've got to be able to throw daggers with accuracy."

"Yeah, guess I'm good at that, too," responded Jacob with mock humility.

They came to a clearing in the trees. They had beaten most of the class. Billy stared at Mrs Trumpet. She looked terrifying with her green mohican and black hoops lining her ears. He would never want to mess with her. Part of him wondered how someone so scary could be married. She was huge; not fat, but like a weight lifter.

He was surprised archery was her speciality, when she would be better at hand-to-hand combat by the size of her. She would be able to crush someone between finger and thumb. That was a slight exaggeration, but the woman had muscles!

"OK, if you've not got your own arrows, grab a set from over there." Mrs Trumpet pointed to a rack of bows and a wooden crate of arrows. Her voice was oddly feminine and high for her appearance, thought Billy; not what he was expecting.

Jacob returned to Billy's side with a well-worn wooden bow and some blue arrows. "Boy, I had to get in quick to get the blue ones," he stated.

"Does the colour of the arrows matter?" He looked at his own black ones with concern.

"Well, no, but I didn't want to end up with pink ones, did I?"

"Why not?"

"Pink's for girls, ain't it?"

Billy laughed. "Think that's a bit of a stereotype, Jacob."

"Maybe, but look at Jake laughing at Jeremy's pink arrows...not everyone is above stereotyping like you, Mate."

"Jacob! Billy! When you've finished chatting, you will be my first contestants!"

Yet again, teachers knew their names without introduction.

"I suggest you pay close attention," said Mrs Trumpet looking over the top of her rectangular glasses.

She picked up the bow with her left hand, "Pick the bow up with your non-dominant hand with the string closest to you. Bend your fingers around the grip." She demonstrated and the class copied. "Your thumb should rest on the back of the bow grip and your index finger should wrap around the front. Hold the bow perpendicular to the ground."

"What's that mean?" whispered Jacob.

"Hold it at a right-angle to the ground...just copy what you see," replied Billy.

"Keep your hand relaxed, but steady," continued Mrs Trumpet.

She turned from facing the class to the circular target in the distance. "Line your body up perpendicular to the target...are you sensing a theme, class?"

Billy and the others copied her including her stance, but she clarified that their feet needed to be shoulder width apart.

"Stand upright!" she pointed her bow down, placed the shaft of an arrow on the arrow rest of the bow and attached the back of the arrow to the string. "One feather should point away from the bow." She held the bow up towards the target, "Use three fingers to lightly hold the arrow on the string and use your thumb to support the back of the arrow and keep it straight. Your inner elbow should be parallel to the ground."

Billy was enjoying archery immensely already. The math references made things easier to understand for him. Unfortunately, the same couldn't be said for Jacob, whose arrow kept dropping. To be fair to him, he wasn't the only one having difficulties; Malyssa was getting her fingers in a right muddle on the string. Billy wondered if he was the only one who had noticed that three out of four of Mrs Trumpet's fingers were below the arrow; not evenly split with two above and two below like they all seemed to be doing...except Jake, who also seemed to be doing well in this lesson.

"Draw the string back as far as possible to increase accuracy," called Mrs Trumpet over her shoulder. "Point the tip of your arrow towards the target, and...relax the fingers on your string hand to release the arrow." She did exactly that. Her arrow whooshed through the air and hit the centre of the target with a solid 'chunk', followed by a chorus of, "WOW!" from the class.

"You're up, Jacob, Billy!" She whistled to them too, and nodded her head towards where they needed to stand.

Billy stepped up confidently with his bow already in his left hand. He took up the stance with his feet shoulder width apart. He applied the mathematical techniques, mumbling them as he carried them out. Jacob was trying his best to copy him, but without much joy.

Billy released the arrow: TWANG, WHOOSH, THUD! It was over quickly. He looked at Jacob's target; he'd at least hit the target. His arrow sat in the white outer ring, furthest from the centre. He looked back at his own. The black arrow with blue feathers protruded just off centre. A hush came over the children when they realised.

"Very good, Billy! Um...Jacob, better luck on your next two arrows," said Mrs Trumpet, "Get ready to fire again."

No-one watched Jacob this time, which took some of the pressure off of him and planted it on Billy. They all stared at his target with great anticipation. His second arrow flew swiftly through the air, and landed just to the left of centre instead of the right this time. Nobody noticed Jacob's land in the trees beyond the target.

"Excellent!" cried Mrs Trumpet, "One more!"

He pulled back the string, and just as he was letting go a large black blob rustled in the trees ahead and he swore he heard the caw of a crow. His arrow sailed up into the air and into the trees as he screeched in shock. Jake led the class in a raucous of laughter.

Billy looked around at his class. There were only a handful of children not laughing. Albeit; most of those laughing were just caught up in its infectious nature, but it was still too much for Billy to handle. He took off through the woods away from the class. Tears streamed down his face. He couldn't work out whether they were tears of sadness or anger; he felt both. He found a small, quiet opening by a pond and began lobbing stones into it as hard as he could. With each throw he felt his emotions stabilising.

Suddenly, a body thrust itself into the small opening too. Billy got ready to throw more stones at it until he realised it was Malyssa. He was about to tell her to leave him alone until he saw her teary eyes.

"Did Jake laugh at you too?" He asked, handing her a stone.

"Laugh? He humiliated me!" She tossed the stone into the pond, and Billy handed her another.

"What did he do?"

She shuffled her feet in the fallen leaves and didn't look up. "He told everyone that I had a crush on you."

"Don't worry about it...at least you didn't scream at a shadow!" he kicked the sticks nearest him.

"He kept going on and on and I couldn't concentrate and my arrows didn't hit the target...not one! He started telling me again that I'm an embarrassment to The Gifted Academy."

"What a jerk!" said Billy, "What did Mrs Trumpet say?"

"She was telling him off when I ran off."

"Good!"

Malyssa changed the subject, "You know no-one is going to remember your screaming, they'll be too busy talking about your bull's eyes, so don't be too upset."

"Really?"

"Yeah, you should have heard Mrs Trumpet talk about you when you left. She said you're a natural...like your mother." Her voice trailed off.

"Huh? My mother did archery?"

"Apparently so. And she was good too."

146

Billy leant against a nearby tree, contemplating the newest information. "Was Jake good at archery?" He didn't know why he was interested, but he was.

"You know he would have been. He trains all the time in all the combatant classes. I heard him telling those friends of his about his mum buying him training equipment. What a mamma's boy!"

Billy laughed. Malyssa was right; Jake came across tough but he was definitely a 'mamma's boy'. Malyssa was laughing too. It was nice, thought Billy, laughing with someone rather than being laughed at or worse...still being completely ignored like you don't exist, which is what he was used to.

In the other world he sat alone, ate alone, played alone, and was never given the chance for sports lessons because the other children didn't want to play with him because they thought he was weird. Turns out they were right! He was weird, but there were loads of people just as weird as him.

"How are you so good?" Malyssa asked him curiously. It was like she'd been reading his thoughts.

"I have no idea. I've never done this sort of thing. My sports lessons consisted of sitting out to the side reading a book, whilst the others played."

"Didn't your teacher mind?"

"Not really. I guess they saw I was happy with a book and left me to it."

"Were you?"

"Was I what?" Billy asked confused.

"Happy?" Malyssa probed.

"Yes. I think so. I could escape my rubbish life in a book. People like Jake never win in a story."

"He's not winning now either!" stated Malyssa.

"Of course he is! He's had us both in tears, been top in Manifesting lesson and probably archery too."

"Yes, but you annoyed him in maths by finishing so quickly and you were able to manifest without any prior knowledge and you have a natural talent at archery. You've done great in all three lessons we've had!"

Billy looked at Malyssa. She beamed as she told him these facts.

"As your friend," said Malyssa, "I'm telling you: don't waste your time comparing yourself to Jake. And never think of him as better than you. I've not known either of you long and I can already tell I chose my friends wisely when I started talking to you yesterday." She blushed, but Billy didn't know why. He was just happy to have such a considerate friend.

In a moment of complete honesty, Billy told Malyssa, "You and Jacob are great! I've not had friends before."

Malyssa didn't ask why, or laugh, but replied, "Well, there's a lot of people out there that have missed out then." Followed by another wide smile. She tucked a few strands of loose blonde hair behind her ears. She checked her watch.

"If we run now we can be first to the cafeteria for lunch." She started running before Billy even had a chance to respond.

They were a few minutes early. However, slowly but surely, other children began to arrive. They let the bigger guys go first and waited for the rest of their class, discussing the lunch possibilities.

Jake led the way, of course. He put his hands to his face and pretended to scream silently. Only Billy and Malyssa saw, it wasn't even for his cronies' amusement. Jake shoulder bumped Billy as he went past him. Jacob came running towards them, "Mate, you were unreal back there!"

"Huh?" *Was he referring to the screaming and running away?*

"Yeah, had you not been startled, I reckon your last arrow would have been a bull's eye too!"

149

He patted Billy on the back, "We've been talking about it since the lesson finished." Jacob joined the lunch queue and Billy and Malyssa followed.

"Who's 'we'?"

"All of us. Well, except Jake and his lot, but they were too busy praising Jake for getting the highest score."

"Of course he did," mumbled Billy.

But Jacob heard him, "Don't get jealous, Mate."

"I'm not jealous," said Billy defensively, "Just getting fed up with him, that's all."

"There's people like him everywhere, don't let him get you down, especially after how well you did!"

Jacob held out a tray as the dinner lady placed some gravy over his vegetables. "Thanks," he said to her. He waited for Billy to get his food, still talking. "We reckon you'd have won, seriously! Mrs Trumpet thinks you're amazing. She kept going on about you."

"Wasn't she mad I'd runaway?" Billy was nervous about the answer.

"She didn't seem to be. Think she was too pleased with your skills." He pulled a funny face, "She wasn't too pleased with mine though." Billy started laughing. Jacob had such a carefree attitude to everything and a brilliant ability to be able to laugh at himself.

"You've aced all today's lessons so far. Wonder what you'll be like this afternoon...hope you're on my team if we go by this morning's skill."

Malyssa had parted ways with them to sit with Jeremy in the Air House section.

Jacob and Billy sat at an empty table, which probably wouldn't stay that way for long. Jacob continued to talk between mouthfuls of roast potatoes, "Can't wait for next lesson! I'm good at it!"

"What is it?" Billy still hadn't looked at his timetable.

"Footy!"

"Oh, cool!" Billy may not have played with the other kids, but he played in the garden with a leather ball Mr Scott had given him.

"You like football?" asked Jacob.

"Of course!" Billy was definitely brightening.

"Who do you support?"

He didn't really support anyone because he didn't watch football, but he'd seen some of the kids with hats and scarves at school, "Arsenal". He said, hoping he'd picked right, the same as his friend.

"Oh, they're good, but they're in the other realm." He shoved some meat-free chicken between his lips and swallowed after barely chewing. "What about this realm?"

"There's different teams in this realm?"

"Oh, sorry, of course, you don't know about this realm do you?" he asked rhetorically.

Billy just looked wide-eyed at him, an expression he was used to having in this realm.

"I support Ocean Giants! They're the best! Of course, I was always going to support a mainly water team, but they're the best anyway. Currently top of the league!"

Billy had no idea what Jacob was talking about.

"Do you play football?" Jacob asked.

"I'm OK, pretty skilled, but not played with others...unless my sister counts." He laughed at himself this time.

"But, you've not played it *here*, have you?"

"No. Is there a difference?"

"Yeah! Just a bit, Mate! But, you'll love it! Trust me!"

"You've played?" Billy asked.

Jacob put down his cutlery, "Well...no...because you can't before going to an academy here… but I've watched tonnes on TV!"

Chapter Nine

Football with a Twist

Billy loved walking from class to class through the woodlands. As he, Jacob and Malyssa walked and talked about what Billy could expect from the following lesson, the sun kept breaking through the trees and blinding him every other second.

Malyssa and Jacob debated their favourite football teams. Malyssa's was obviously a predominantly Air Team, just as Jacob's was biased towards Water players. Billy understood barely any of what they were saying and he certainly wasn't prepared for what lay before him.

"Are you kidding me?" He suddenly burst out with when he saw the pitch. He knew sometimes pitches got water logged from heavy rainfall, but this was ridiculous; there was more water than there was grass. "We can't play on that! You can't even see the grass under the water!"

Jacob and Malyssa looked at one another and smirked, "Do you want to tell him or shall I?" Malyssa asked Jacob.

"Tell me what?"

"I'll tell him," said Jacob.

"OK, go ahead."

"So, there's not any grass under that water, Mate. Think of those as lakes or pools."

"Lakes!" you don't have lakes or pools in the middle of football pitches!"

"We do here!" chimed in Malyssa.

"This is an awesome version of football, Mate, seriously! It takes into account that we have gifts of manifestation, skills that the regular footballers don't have...well not many of them, and they certainly can't use them there. In this game you've got to be a skilled Manifestus or you won't last two minutes."

"So, I can change into part frog?" He asked for clarification.

"Yeah, and full frog, and whatever else you are...at some point."

Maybe it would *be a better football game,* thought Billy.

"This is only the 5-a-side pitch, wait 'till you see the real pitch for academy teams."

"You have more than one school team?" Billy rubbed his chin.

"Yeah, we can have a bit of a competition in school and the winning team gets a trophy."

"And as an academy, we get to watch all the games!" added Malyssa.

"The two teams have existed as long as the academy has," explained Jacob, "It's a huge honour to make the teams... either one. They play other academies too." Up until Jacob said that, Billy had completely forgotten there were more academies.

"We're only first years, surely we won't make a team with Sixth Formers?" said Billy trying to work out why Jacob and Malyssa were so excited about something that's not really relevant to them.

"That's the thing: age doesn't matter when it comes to gifts and talents. If the teachers think you've got talent, you'll be drafted. It's as simple as that!"

"So, you want to play for the team?" asked Billy.

"Not me," replied Malyssa, "I'm happy watching. I'd rather get involved in music."

"But I do! For sure!" cried Jacob. "I want to go pro! The kits are awesome!"

Billy rolled his eyes and smiled, "You just want the money!"

"There isn't money in pro football here...well, not like in normal football anyway."

"Gather round me!" called Mr Leadbetter. Billy was pleased that Mr Leadbetter was teaching football, at least he sort of knew him.

"Put your boots on please." Bags swung to the grass, and there was a lot more chatter as the children replaced their chunky boots with football boots. Although they were a little different to the ones Billy was used to. His boots were navy blue leather with sky blue wavy lines on and studded on the bottom, like usual. But, from the foot hole was a sort of canvas fabric that continued to be laced. He wore what looked like high-top football boots. Jacob's feet were long and narrow in the football boots and made him look like he had clown feet.

"Whoa, Billy! Nice boots!" stated Gerard. His own boots were a dull green and muddy brown, "They must have cost a bit!"

"Oh, um, thanks. I have no idea what they cost, Miss Leadbetter paid for them." Gerard looked shocked and

Billy realised his mistake, "No, no, she paid out of my money. I just meant she chose them."

"She's got good taste! They're top of the line." He looked at Jacob's, which were not and gave him a friendly half-smile, "Don't worry, Jacob, mine aren't much better than yours...did your mum pick yours out too?"

Jacob looked at the floor and shuffled from side to side. "These were Peter's, my older brother's. He out grew them."

Fortunately, Mr Leadbetter interrupted the awkward conversation, "Everyone done?" He looked at all their feet, even though he heard a mass response of 'yes!'

"Great! I'm going to sort you into seven groups of five, that leaves one spare, but that's OK, I can swap you in. And there's no use begging me for changes because I worked out the groups prior to this lesson to keep things fair." A few children groaned, but most stayed silent waiting in anticipation for who their team Mates would be.

"Group one, stand together when I call your names: Daniel, Georgie, Bethan, Frankie and Joybella." He didn't even give them time to grumble before he called out the next group, "Savannah, Paris, Isaiah, Aavar and Irene. Three: Simon, James," the twins high-fived one another,

"Jeremy, Ria and Cheryl." Billy bit his fingernails. Mr Leadbetter continued, "Four: Blossom, Joseph, Stella, Jacob and Spike."

Billy was getting nervous, he really didn't want to be in a team with Jake again. He listened intently to the group five's names, "Skylar, Jake," there it was; Jake had been called.

Billy mumbled to himself repeatedly, "Please don't say my name! Please don't say my name!"

"Quinn," continued Mr Leadbetter barely pausing for breath, "Mary and..." Time seemed to stand still for Billy, "...Alfie."

"Yes!" yelled Billy. The rest of the class shot him a confused glance. He turned a lovely shade of red. Billy wasn't in the next group either.

"And last but by no means least, team seven will be Malyssa, Billy, Rachel, Zachary and India. That should give every team a fair chance. Aron, I'll switch you in."

"OK, let's see what we have before any teaching, shall we?" he asked rhetorically. He pointed at teams one and two, "Ones you're playing up the pitch; twos you're playing down! Go! Be ready for the whistle. You've got five minutes before we switch round and you play the other way!"

Billy looked out to the pitch wondering where on earth the players stood for kick off. He watched Frankie and Aavar stand in the centre circle. Bethan ran up to the rest of her team with red bibs before standing in the wing on the far side of the pitch and Joybella stood in the other wing, the body of water on their half of the pitch separating them. Daniel stood on the grass in the wing behind Bethan, and Georgie was in goal.

Paris handed out yellow bibs to her team and then stood opposite Bethan on the far side, Irene behind her level with the roped off section in the water marking the semi-circle penalty area. Savannah stood in the wing closest to where Billy was viewing. He was surprised to see how interested all the girls were in the game compared to his old school. Everyone on both teams was focussed. Isaiah stood in goal, his afro reaching the cross bar. Neither goalie wore gloves.

Mr Leadbetter walked to the centre and placed a white leather football on the centre mark and walked back to the edge of the pitch. He was limping. The whistle rang sharp in Billy's ears and Aavar tapped the ball to his right before pelting it to Paris who blasted the ball towards the goal, where Georgie easily caught it. He kicked the ball high into the air towards Bethan, who kicked it across the water to Joybella, who toe-punted it at the goal, where Isaiah was ready and waiting.

The game continued in both halves much the same way: everybody avoiding the ball landing in the water. They were very skilled, but Billy couldn't help wondering why they have the water, (besides making it harder to play), it didn't really add anything to the game. In fact, players didn't even seem to tackle one another. Maybe the next game would be more interesting between teams three and four.

Sadly not; well, at least not in the way a sport should be interesting. It did get interesting when Jacob made a spectacular dive for the ball just as the whistle blew at the end of the second half and landed in the water. But, still, Billy couldn't see what was so special about football here.

Mr Leadbetter called them off the pitch and then it was Jake's team in red and Billy's team in yellow. Billy had no idea where he was supposed to stand and hung back until the others had taken up positions. "How do they know where to stand without talking to each other?" he mumbled, but Mr Leadbetter caught it.

"It's a game of not just skill, but instinct. Remember that, Billy, my little water baby!" He gave Billy a wink, who went to stand in the wing.

Mr Leadbetter blew the whistle for kick off. The ball spent most of its time down Billy's end of the pitch where it snuck past Malyssa in goal. Team Five cheered, especially Jake who looked at Billy smugly.

Billy wasn't playing very skilfully. He was too busy watching the ground to avoid falling in the water. He didn't want to do that! What use would he be in there? And that's when he realised what Mr Leadbetter had said and why he winked.

The teams switched ends. This time when the ball flew high into the air, Billy didn't stay on the ground, he leapt high into the air to meet the ball before falling into the water with a splash and reappearing with the ball caught in a webbed foot. He flung his leg forward and released the ball, which flew into the back of the net past a disgruntled Jake. Most people were cheering, including Mr Leadbetter, who yelled, "At a boy!"

Jake booted the ball over the centre of the pitch and Billy followed it into the water on the opposite side to where he'd been. He threw the ball with a webbed foot out to Rachel, who passed it to India, who kicked it to Zachary, who passed it back to Billy, who was back in the water closest to Jake. He made to look like he was going to fling the ball in the goal, which Jake dived for, but Billy blasted the ball to Zachary on the left, and he booted the ball into the back of an empty goal.

The children roared with cheers! Jake roared with anger. He'd been made to look the fool twice now. *Why didn't he manifest?*

Mr Leadbetter blew the final whistle and the children screamed with delight chanting Billy's name. Jake scowled whilst a doting Quinn and Cheryl tried to console him. He pushed the girls away and stomped off.

"Billy, my boy!" yelled Mr Leadbetter as he limped over to him. Billy's hair and top half of clothes dripped on the grass. Mr Leadbetter tousled Billy's hair, flicking a few spots of water around, "You were amazing! I knew you'd be great!"

Billy blushed, not used to the attention and certainly not this amount of high praise.

"I sincerely hope you will try-out for the school team!"

"D-don't you have a team already?" Billy stammered.

"Each year there are new try-outs. You stand a great chance of making the team if you play like that!" He flung his leg forward pretending to kick a ball and winced.

"What have you done to your leg, Sir?" asked Billy concerned.

"Um, nothing really. Just a football injury."

"You should get Malyssa to take a look at it, she's a bee and she can heal stuff. She healed my face yesterday." He looked around for Malyssa who was on her way towards him. Billy beckoned for her to come closer.

"No, no, I don't need it looked at," he said twisting the ring on his left index finger.

Billy ignored him, "Malyssa, can you heal Mr Leadbetter's leg?"

"Of course I can." She bent down and placed her hands on his lower leg, before he could move. He pulled his leg away abruptly, "I said 'no'!" he was very firm and stared deep into Billy's eyes. Billy felt himself shrinking back. He wasn't expecting it. Malyssa kept silent.

"I need to go," stated Mr Leadbetter before limping away across the pitch to the woods on the far side that Billy hadn't been to yet. "CLASS DISMISSED!"

"Why wouldn't he let you heal it?"

"Billy..." said Malyssa.

"Why was he so suddenly cross with me when I was trying to help?"

"Billy..." Malyssa repeated.

Billy stared after Mr Leadbetter paying no attention to Malyssa. "I thought he liked me..."

"Billy!" shouted Malyssa, this time getting his

attention.

"What?" He still didn't look round.

"Look!" she commanded.

Billy turned swiftly and looked at her not sure of what he was looking at, until she held up her hands. They were red.

"Is that blood?" asked Billy.

"Yes, it seeped through his trousers. He must have a bad cut, because my hands barely touched his leg." Her brow wrinkled.

"Hey Billy! You were amazing!" Jacob patted him on the back before looking in the direction Billy was, who hadn't responded to the compliment. He saw Malyssa's red hands. "Is that blood?" His lip curled and he gulped.

"Yes, it's from Mr Leadbetter's leg. It's why he was limping."

"I don't like blood," Jacob whined looking away and breathing deeply.

"Go wash your hands in the pitch's water," suggested Billy.

"Good idea." Malyssa walked away.

"She's gone to wash them now. Better, Jacob?" Billy rested a gentle hand on Jacob's shoulder. Jacob was bent over unsure if he would be sick, "You were still amazing," murmured Jacob.

Billy laughed, "Thanks, *Mate*."

Malyssa returned drying her hands on her trousers.

"Where's Mr Leadbetter gone?" asked Billy, looking in the general direction Mr Leadbetter had walked in.

"I don't know what's over there," replied Malyssa, "according to the academy's map, it's just woodland and then the moat around the grounds." She paused and looked first at Jacob and then at Billy as an idea formed in her mind, "We could follow him and find out..."

"Follow a teacher?" asked Jacob, "Doesn't sound like a good idea." He stood straight, the queasy feeling having passed.

"But he's hurt, Jacob and he's gone off to the woodlands alone. What if he passes out from blood loss?"

"He's a grown man, Malyssa," stated Jacob.

"That may be true, but even grown men need help sometimes." She stood with her hands on her hips staring at Jacob waiting for his next negative remark.

"I say we go!" said Billy, much to Jacob's surprise, "Come on, Jacob, he needs help, I'm sure of it."

"Oh man! Peer pressure...fine, let's go." He rubbed a hand over his head.

"OK, he's just reached the edge of the woods and he's slow from limping," said Malyssa, "If we run we should be able to catch up but stay far enough away that he doesn't spot us."

"You're good at this," stated Jacob.

"Well, I spy on my older sister a lot and believe me, you don't want her catching you doing that!"

"Come on!" Billy grabbed one arm each of Malyssa and Jacob.

They ran across the pitch and slipped and slid on the wet grass having changed out of their studded boots back into their clumpy ones. They continued sprinting until they reached the edge of the woods. Someone repeatedly walking the same way had worn a narrow path. And they followed the path silently through the trees.

After a while they came to a wooden hut. It was dishevelled. There was a half-rotten step leading to a warped doorframe. Dead leaves and twigs covered a drooping roof. Wild flowers grew all around it.

The building and its land were surrounded by barbed wire. "That must be how he caught his leg," whispered Malyssa, "So be careful when going through the gaps."

Jacob grabbed her as she went through, "You can't go in there. Are you crazy?"

"Why not?"

"For one: there's a sign hanging on the fence saying 'KEEP OUT' in big red letters and two:...it doesn't look safe."

Malyssa looked at him in disbelief. "I'm sure Mr Leadbetter went in there. Look at the tracks, there's not other worn paths."

"She's right, Jacob. Maybe we can just go look through the window."

"OK, that seems fine...I guess."

They squeezed through the gaps in the fencing being careful not to get scratched too badly. They inevitably got scratched a bit. They walked cautiously towards the door and ducked, creeping around to the window on the left.

The window was fairly murky, but they could see Mr Leadbetter inside pacing on the floorboards.

"Tell me where he is!" He suddenly yelled at someone else in the cabin. Billy squinted trying to see better through the dirty windows. Finally, he could see someone sitting in a wooden chair. It was a man dressed head to toe in black, mostly leather. Long black greasy hair hung by his face that had an equally long black greasy beard. The man cackled.

"I said: where is he?"

The man laughed menacingly and then coughed. Mr Leadbetter picked up a piece of wood and threw it at the wall in frustration. It landed on the floor kicking up a cloud of dust.

Mr Leadbetter calmed himself and spoke softer. Billy could just about hear him. "I know you follow The Beast, we both know that, don't we?"

The man in the chair snarled, but said nothing.

"I know you know where he is! Is he near?"

No response.

Mr Leadbetter slicked back his blue hair that was wringing with sweat. "If he's near, I'll get him, just like I caught you! He's stupid just like you!"

The insult to his pride did it. "You'll never get him!" screeched the greasy man, "He's far too powerful to be caught!"

"Unlike you, who is weak enough to be caught you mean?" Mr Leadbetter got right up close into the man's face as he growled back at him. "How could The Beast have someone as weak and pathetic as you as one of his closest henchmen?"

The man writhed in his chair gritting his teeth.

"Do you expect him to send help for you? To risk someone else for *you?* Is it really likely? Don't you remember how you got your position as his lead henchman, Brutus? Did he save the last life or his own?"

Brutus growled.

"You chose the wrong side, but you can always return to us." He walked round the back and mouthed words by Brutus' ear. Billy could just about lip read them. "We would welcome you back. We still love you, no matter what you've become, Brutus, my dear brother."

Chapter Ten
The Leadbetters

Billy's mouth dropped open. He was pretty sure he made an audible gasp and dropped down below the window. Jacob and Malyssa followed suit. They lent their backs against the moss-covered wood, breathing heavily.

"We need to go now," whispered Malyssa, keeping low, but already moving towards the path leading back to the barbed-wire fence. Jacob went next, it was a lot more effort to keep low for a boy so tall. They had both reached the path and looked back expecting Billy to be behind them, but he was still crouched down by the hut.

Jacob went to go back for him, but Malyssa grabbed his arm, "No, I'll go, it's easier. You make your way to the fence and keep out of view of the windows."

Jacob hesitated briefly, but the distinctive call of an owl's hoot startled him and got him moving.

Having reached Billy, Malyssa touched his arm gently, "We have to go, Billy." He didn't respond.

"Billy, I know you're in shock, but if we get caught you'll be in trouble too, so please, I'm begging, let's get moving." She kept her voice quiet but urgent. Still no response.

There was a loud crash from inside the barn, which seemed to break Billy out of the trance like state he was in.

"Go!" Malyssa whispered gently but firmly nudging him towards the path. Finally, he got up and keeping low, ran across the dead leaves covering the path and zipped between the gap in the barbed-wire fence that Jacob had made bigger by holding it open. Malyssa followed.

They ran through the woodland path, weaving in and out of trees and made it out to the open field. Jacob was about to run towards the 5-a-side football pitch, the same way they had come, but Malyssa stopped him, "No! Mr Leadbetter will probably take the most obvious route." She pointed to a patch of trees leading back into the main woodland around the academy. "It will take us a lot longer, but we are less likely to be caught by Mr Leadbetter."

Neither of the boys had to be talked into it. All three children sprinted towards the trees Malyssa had pointed out. As they ran, not one of them looked back to see if Mr Leadbetter had come out of the woods yet.

Eventually they stopped running and hid behind trees to catch their breath and to look back across the green field. They could not see him. Billy breathed a sigh of relief and leant his back against the tree he hid behind, resting his head too.

"It's quite a long way back and we'll probably have to make our way straight to the cafeteria for dinner or we'll miss it," said Malyssa.

Jacob groaned at the prospect of missing dinner. "Are we ready to move on?" asked Jacob, "Billy, you doing OK?"

"That horrible man in there is related to the Leadbetters?"

"Apparently, yes," replied Malyssa un-phased.

"Did you know they had a brother?" asked Billy. He didn't move from the tree.

"We knew they *had* a brother but it was reported that he died years ago."

"Died? How?"

"In a fire. They couldn't find the remains. The building and everything in it were just ash."

"Probably around ten years ago. We were babies. I just remember Mum singing the Leadbetter family praises when she saw my birthmark start showing," said Jacob.

"She sung *all* their praises?" Billy was flabbergasted. He couldn't believe they had praised that thing in there; he wasn't even a person really. Billy recalled the pointed nose and sharp talon like fingers and pitch black eyes. Even in human form Brutus resembled a bird.

The three of them made their way through the woods. How Malyssa knew where she was going Billy didn't know, there was no worn path, no trail, but she led them confidently through the tall trees rising out of the earth brushing the sky.

The sun was beginning to set and the sweat on Billy's body was cooling dramatically. He shivered as he followed Malyssa and Jacob, continuing his questions.

"Why was Brutus in a fire?"

"He saved someone...I don't know really. I only remember snippets my mum told me. Jacob, do you know more?"

Jacob shrugged, "No, only that he's remembered as a

hero. I can't even remember who he was meant to have saved."

"We've got to tell Miss Leadbetter that Brutus is alive and that he's here!" stated Billy emphatically.

"We can't tell anyone, Billy!" replied Malyssa.

"Why?"

"We weren't supposed to be there. We aren't supposed to know. We will be in big trouble!"

"But this is a big deal, Malyssa! She would want to know her brother is alive!" Billy insisted.

"I agree with Malyssa, Mate," added Jacob, "And what makes you think she doesn't already know? She's Headmistress of this academy!"

Billy couldn't believe what he was hearing. They thought Miss Leadbetter knew that Brutus was on the academy grounds and was allowing it. It couldn't be! She wouldn't put the children in danger, surely? He didn't know why he felt so defensive of Miss Leadbetter. Maybe it was because she's already shown him so much kindness, but then so had Mr Leadbetter, but he knew about Brutus. He was the one keeping him here, locked in a flimsy, rotting, wooden hut.

Billy rubbed the back of his neck. "Maybe you're right, maybe we shouldn't say anything...at least not without more knowledge."

"We've got other things to worry about anyway," said Jacob a lot more cheerfully than they had been talking so far.

"We do? What?"

"Yeah! It's football try-outs next week!" Jacob had a new bounce to his walk thinking about it.

"You seem excited about them rather than worried. Are you not a little worried?" asked Malyssa.

"Nah, 'course I'm not worried. I play football all the time, and I'm practically the same height as some of the older kids...I'd be an excellent goalie!"

Billy took a sideways glance as Jacob pretended to save an imaginary ball and then ran around cheering, "The crowd goes wild! He's done it again! Jacob Sole, the world's best goal keeper!"

Malyssa and Billy fell about laughing, which had the extra benefit of warming Billy up.

As time went on hunger made them quieter. They walked silently to the cafeteria, joined their Houses for dinner and tired after an eventful day, they went straight back to their dormitories to rest.

The evening before try-outs arrived. Jacob and Billy decided, like everyone else trying-out for the football teams, to get an early night. Most people in all the year groups went to bed by about nine o'clock.

After another long day Billy was shattered by the time he had climbed the twirling staircase to the Year Seven's dormitories. He dragged himself over to the edge of his bed, changed into his two-tone blue pyjamas, his fingers fumbling over the buttons, and fell into his sleeping bag without brushing his teeth. His bedroom fell silent quickly as most of the boys wanted to try-out for the football team, and even those that didn't were going to watch anyway, so as to not be the odd one out in knowing what happened.

Billy closed his eyes expecting to drift off into dreamland fairly swiftly, but sleep eluded him. The hours seemed to tick by and all he seemed to do was toss and turn. He could hear a number of the boys snoring, some louder than he would have liked. He squeezed the pillow over his ears trying to drown them out, but it was of no use.

He stared at the timber beams above his head and the wooden panel supporting Lesley as he slept in the storage area above. He listened to the squeak of the metal camp bed frame and the quiet mutterings that were indecipherable coming from a sleep talking Lesley. Billy chuckled.

Suddenly, an owl hooted. Billy jumped. His heart raced as he was drawn back to last week's events over at the dilapidated cabin. He could once again smell the damp rotting wood and musty earth. He could feel the rotten wood of the windowsill they were peering through crumbling beneath his fingers. As he recalled the memories, it was as if an enhanced video was playing in his mind. All his senses seemed heightened, and he recalled things that weren't apparent to him earlier in the day. His mind must have taken in and stored more than he realised. The memories had repeated on him for over a week.

He saw the fireplace filled with ash and blackened wood blocks; a rickety wooden bench. When the owl had made him jump at the cabin and he sat frozen staring into the wilderness in front of the cabin leading to the barbed-wire fence, he could make out animal tracks in the mud near by. He felt the spider web hanging below the windowsill tickling his face. As he lay in his bed, he ruffled his hair hopefully removing the web. He shuddered and drew back into the dormitory.

He closed his eyes and tried to rest the best he could until light shone through the blue curtains indicating morning.

Eventually, the boys began to stir. He heard Jacob roll over and fiddle with items on his bedside cabinet. It rattled and clinked as he picked up various items and placed them back down until he found what he wanted.

"Six fifty four," Jacob mumbled. He yawned loudly whilst muttering, "Six minutes left..." He stretched and then relaxed and lay still for another six minutes.

Alarms went off at seven o'clock, left, right and centre in the dormitory. Bobby opposite him, sat bolt upright confused and dazed, his brown hair that normally hung roughly against his forehead was now more resembling a bird's nest. Isaac, a small red-headed boy, groaned.

Billy stayed where he was, watching the scene un-fold. He was repaid handsomely for his observation when Jacob flung back his sleeping bag, leapt to the floor landing with a crash and began to sing and dance whilst getting ready. (The term singing being used loosely.) "It's football try-outs! Yay! I'm going to be on the team! Yay!"

Billy sat up and laughed at this gangly boy, making an awful noise whilst getting his clothes on. "You not showering?" asked Billy, a smile beaming across his face.

"No point!" replied Jacob pulling his faded navy cardigan over his head covering his tunic. Obviously, Billy wasn't the only one too lazy to undo the buttons. It was also obvious that a family member had handed it down to Jacob. James and Simon also wore faded ones yesterday, a little stretched in places too. "Only going to need another one after the spectacular saves I make today!" He continued, "For now, it's shower in a can!" And he proceeded to spray himself heavily with deodorant. Billy laughed even more and choked a little on the spray.

The rest of the boys were getting dressed without showering too, probably for the same reason, although he knew, being a boy himself, he wasn't about to rush for the shower anyway, try-outs or no try-outs. Billy decided to get dressed too and the whole of the boys' dormitory made their way to the cafeteria. A few of the girls joined them too.

It was a bright day but nippy and Billy was still not adjusted to the cooler weather. The wind blew through his curls.

"Why are none of the other boys in our House up?" asked Billy.

"Year Sevens are up first for try-outs," Jacob replied.

"Look ahead you can see the other year sevens going in. There's Jeremy and Zachary." He pointed to a small boy with green tints in his slicked-back dark hair. Billy was amazed, back in his old school if a child dyed their hair any colour other than one considered natural he'd have been sent home and made to cut it off...even if it meant shaving the head...including the girls! It didn't happen too often, but in this realm it was as common for someone to have dyed hair, as it was to wear glasses in the other realm. Albeit, there wasn't too many in his year, but they were used to the old school systems.

"Hey! Look! There's Malyssa!" said Jacob. "Malyssa!"

Malyssa was approaching the steps to the main building but stopped when she saw it was them calling her name.

"Hi guys!"

"I didn't expect to see you up this early and going to try-outs," said Jacob, not making eye contact. The meaning behind his comment that she was not very good at football was apparent to all three of them without stating the obvious.

"I know I'm not good," stated Malyssa flicking her hair in annoyance, just in case they thought she was too stupid to understand, "But Billy is and I wanted to support him and see the look on Jake's stupid face when Billy makes a team and he doesn't!" She smirked.

"What about me making the team?" He looked at her wide-eyed. His words were scratchy.

Malyssa realised he didn't mean to hurt her feelings and changed her tone towards him, "Yes, I'm sure you'll do brilliant too."

"Thanks, Malyssa! Come watch us both!" requested Jacob.

"I will cheer you both on and I'm just proud of you even if you don't make a team." Jacob wasn't looking at her anymore. He focussed on the breakfast counter coming up trying to see over the shoulders of others to see what was on offer, but Billy watched Malyssa aim the comment about not making the team solely at Jacob.

Billy picked up a clear plastic food tray and slid it along the metal counters. He wasn't particularly hungry, not even the delicious smell of meat-free sausages could persuade his stomach to eat as much as usual.

Jacob, on the other hand, piled his tray high with not only sausages, but also eggs, tomatoes, beans and mushrooms. Billy did a double take at Jacob's tray.

"You not eating?" Jacob asked Billy looking at his empty tray.

"Think I may just have some toast."

"Ah, grab me a slice whilst you're getting yours!" called Jacob to Billy who was going round those at the serving hatches to the toaster.

"You serious?"

"Yeah, Mate, got to be energised for the try-out!"

Billy shook his head and smiled. He placed a couple of slices of white bread into one of several toasters. Once he'd buttered them he went to join Jacob who had already parted ways with Malyssa. She called him a pig in jest and went to sit with Jeremy.

Billy sat with his back facing the doors into the cafeteria. Jacob nodded his head towards the doors and said something Billy couldn't make out through a mouthful of baked beans.

"Say that again."

"Leadbetter's just come in," repeated Jacob.

Billy turned his head swiftly to the double doors. Mr Leadbetter had joined the queue for food. He shuffled along so slowly. Billy couldn't tell if he was still limping. He watched him receive his egg sandwich and slowly limp his way to the teachers' circular table in the centre of the room. Mr Leadbetter winced as he advanced the steps. He caught Billy's gaze as he sat down to eat.

Billy's heart palpitated and his stomach flipped as Mr Leadbetter fixed him in a stare. His knee started bouncing nervously under the table. *Had Mr Leadbetter seen them yesterday at the cabin?* He put his slice of toast back on the tray taking his eyes off Mr Leadbetter for a split second. When he returned to look upon him Mr Leadbetter was smiling at him. The crow's feet at the corners of his eyes curled up towards his mohican, which was beautifully held in place.

For the first time Billy noticed a partial tattoo above the blue collar of Mr Leadbetter's shirt. He squinted to see it better and Mr Leadbetter pulled his collar up and shuffled in his chair before looking back to his plate where hi eyes remained.

"You not eating the other half of your toast?"

Billy shook his head. Jacob grabbed it and bit into it hungrily, like he hadn't eaten in days. Billy turned back to the teachers' table. Miss Leadbetter had arrived. She looked in Billy's direction smiling whilst whispering into her brother's ear. He too looked up and smiled again at Billy. Billy looked around him pretending to be looking for something.

"Done! Let's go!" Jacob pushed his chair back with his legs and grabbed his and Billy's trays. He looked over towards where Malyssa was sitting at which point she pushed her chair out and joined them by the Round Hall doors.

"Where are the try-outs?" asked Billy.

"5-a-side pitch like our classes."

"Won't it just be a repeat of our lessons then? Hasn't he seen us play?"

"Yeah, maybe...I guess." Jacob had not really thought about it.

The three of them made their way to the pitch. As they got closer and closer they noticed some of the older years were up and about and making their way in the same direction.

"Why are they coming?"

"Maybe they want to check out all the new talent." Jacob puffed out his chest.

Billy jumped as a hand landed on his shoulder.

"Oh sorry there, Billy." It was the boy from year thirteen, the one with the muscles, whose name Billy couldn't remember. "I didn't mean to make you jump." He took his hand away and stood in front of Billy, towering over him.

Billy said nothing, just stared up at him trying to slow his heart rate back to normal.

"I just wanted to say good luck out there! Bring it! And don't worry about us older ones, don't back down!" He jostled Billy's blonde curls. "Mr Leadbetter just told me you're trying-out. He told me you're good!"

"Are you coming to watch the year seven try-outs?" Billy cocked his head to the side.

"Year Seven try-outs? What are you talking about?" He narrowed his eyes at Billy, "We all try-out together. That's why I'm saying don't be put off by us bigger ones." He tugged at the collar of his own tunic. Sports gear looked a lot better on him, the tunic clung to his muscles and the navy combats looked fitted rather than the combination looking like a tent on a scrawny little body like Billy's.

"Be yourself. Leadbetter says you're a natural. I'm looking forward to hopefully playing you...even if it's only try-outs." He winked at Billy, then added, "which I'm sure it won't be." He ran to catch up with a group of boys and girls ahead.

"He knows your name!" said Jacob, his mouth wide and his eyebrows raised.

"Yeah, that's the boy who gave me the tip about taking the central staircase to the dorms." He looked at Jacob who was rubbing his hands on his face wondering if her was dreaming.

"Who is he, again?" asked Billy innocently.

"Who is he? *Who is he?*" Jacob flung his arms in the air and then flung them in the boy's direction, "that's Bradley Jonas!" Jacob watched for the penny to drop, but it didn't.

Billy shrugged half-heartedly. "Am I supposed to know who that is?"

"You don't know?" Jacob was beyond shocked. He looked like his head was about to explode.

"I don't know anything about this place, remember?"

Jacob took a deep breath, "That, Billy, is the younger brother of Owen Jonas, and Owen Jonas is the best footballer ever! He plays for Ocean Giants." He put an arm round Billy's shoulders, "He's going to be joining Ocean Giants as soon as his last year at the academy is over. You, Billy, know a footballer!" He friendly punched Billy in the upper arm, before letting go of him completely and smoothing down his tunic and combat trousers and checking his afro.

"Oh," said Billy nodding, it didn't really mean much to him that Bradley was a celebrity or at least would be. He just thought it was kind of him to take an interest in him; although he had no idea why he would, he wasn't anything special. Only then, while he was playing over what Bradley said to him did it dawn on him what he had said.

"Jacob, we're playing with the older years!"

"What?"

"You said we were playing against other Year Sevens for try-outs!" He clenched his jaw.

"Well...it was only an assumption," he gulped, "Makes sense to do it in year groups, don't you think?" Jacob pulled a sheepish smile. "But you don't need to worry, Bradley told you, you'd be OK."

"No, he didn't, he just said for me to 'bring it' and that Leadbetter said I was good." Billy shook his head, but also found it quite amusing that Jacob had got it *so* wrong.

"He also wished you good luck...that's something, isn't it?"

Billy laughed and grabbed Jacob by the arm leading him towards the pitch, "Come on!"

Chapter Eleven
Trials, Deals and Secrets

"Billy! Glad you could make it!" Mr Leadbetter walked over to him swinging his right leg in pain. He was trying not to show too much pain on his face.

"He seems pleased to see you," whispered Jacob, "He can't have seen us at the cabin."

"Shhh, he might hear you," replied Billy through gritted teeth as he awkwardly tried to talk and smile.

"Miss Leadbetter pointed out you were in your football boots at breakfast, which I was most happy to see!" Mr Leadbetter was beaming. His blue eyes lit up nearly as brightly as his blue mohican catching the morning sun.

"That's why he was grinning and looking at me," mumbled Billy to himself, feeling a little foolish about his concerns at breakfast.

Mr Leadbetter's collar was still up high covering the tattoo on his neck as Billy tried to get a glimpse.

"Where's your bow?" asked Mr Leadbetter looking over Billy's shoulder.

"I-I don't have it...I thought this was football try-outs."

"It is! But we play differently! You know that!"

Billy tugged on his ear. Mr Leadbetter cocked his head, "No-one told you?" Mr Leadbetter asked looking from Billy to Jacob, who seemed to shrink under Mr Leadbetter's glare.

"Sorry, Mate. I keep forgetting you don't know this stuff," said Jacob.

"Have you got your dagger?"

Jacob lifted up his tunic revealing a large dagger in its sheath about his waist.

"Wait! Wait! Wait!" said Billy totally repulsed by the thought of using weapons on his friends, "You attack the other team?" He gulped, wanting to return to the dormitory and forget try-outs. Jacob didn't seem to understand the concern Billy was showing.

"Show him your weapon, Jacob," directed Mr Leadbetter.

Jacob pulled the dagger out of its sheath. Billy expected to see the glint of metal, but he didn't. Instead, he saw a sort of flattened rubber cylinder with a rounded tip. It was quite wide for a dagger.

"The weapon is covered, Billy," said Mr Leadbetter, "No-one is impaled in the game...maybe some bruises, the odd broken bone or concussion...but not impaled."

"Mine isn't very useful unless I'm close enough to tackle and I play goalie anyway," said Jacob looking down at his feet.

Billy took a deep breath as his mind tried to make sense of the new information. "OK, so what do I have instead of normal arrows?" asked Billy.

"Come with me," replied Mr Leadbetter, "I'll show you. We have a few spares around for when some get busted in the games." Billy gulped and followed Mr Leadbetter as he limped to a large wooden box, which Billy hadn't taken any notice of during his lesson the day before. The other children must have been leaning against it and blocking it from view, either that or he didn't open his eyes properly.

"Why haven't we used weapons in our lessons so far?"

asked Billy.

"You're first years and it was your first lesson. You don't generally play with weapons in your first year, so we practice other skills."

"But...we can today?"

"You have to if you want to be on the team."

Billy stopped and rubbed his temples.

"I shouldn't be concerned, most first years don't make the team because they're not used to it, but we give everyone a chance. But, you have a natural talent in archery, as well as manifesting, so you stand an excellent chance today!" He rummaged in the box and came up with a bow, quiver and arrows. The bow and quiver looked similar to Billy's except older, more worn but the arrows had cylindrical rubber stubs on the end; not much smaller than his fist.

"Hold out your hands," ordered Mr Leadbetter, as he dumped it on Billy and walked away.

Billy walked with the weapon parts in his out-stretched arms back to Jacob. Jacob looked at his wide-eyes and took them from Billy, "OK, let's put the arrows in there..." he put them in the quiver, "And let's put this over like this..." he slipped the quiver over Billy's head and Billy naturally put his arm through it so that it was diagonally across his torso. "And you hold this..." he placed the bow in Billy's left hand. "There! All sorted! Jacob grinned at Billy.

All Billy could do was smile back, his eyebrows raised and eyes glossy. He didn't see this going too well.

"You'll do great, Mate! You're good at football and archery. Just do your best. It's no big deal if you don't make the team...there's six more years to try-out!" He patted Billy on the back, "I'll put a good word in for you when I make the team...maybe you could be a sub. They don't use subs, but maybe I could persuade them to start."

The boys and girls lined up around the edge of the 5-a-side pitch. Spectators stood back not to be confused with a player.

Mr Leadbetter started throwing red and yellow bibs at children at random and sending them to the pitch.

"Watch this game! You'll love it!" said Jacob nudging his friend in the side with his elbow in excitement. He seemed to think Billy would love a lot of things that Billy just found confusing at the moment.

Brad was among the first lot to play. Everyone watching cheered as he stepped onto the pitch still pulling on his yellow bib. He swung his quiver over his head. It brushed against his slicked-back blue hair. His muscles bulged as he gripped his bow in his left hand and held an arrow in his right.

"He's an archer too!" Billy was shocked to see that Brad used the same weapon as him. Except, his bow was black with a blue string, his arrows were black with blue rubber ends, and feathers and his quiver was a deep blue leather with a black rim and strap. He waved the arrow at the cheering crowd and nodded his head in a humble greeting.

Another cheer went up as a girl stepped forward with a streak of blue in her black hair. She high-fives Brad as she pulled on a yellow bib. The crowd cried out, "Violet! Violet! Violet!" as she pulled out a rubber cased sword.

"She's also on the same team as Brad for the school!" shouted Jacob over the crowd.

Billy looked on as the children split over the pitch in red and yellow bibs.

"Who's that?" asked Billy pointing at a large boy with a brown pony-tail with a white streak going from his forehead to the tips of his hair. He had a mean, angry face. Even when he smiled at the crowd it looked more like a snarl. He twirled a rubber flailed ball and chain around his head. The crowd were split between booing and cheering. He lapped up the applause and boos equally; if anything, he seemed to enjoy the boos more.

"That's Freddie Gunner, well, Frederick. He's awful! Always plays against Brad."

"If he's awful, why is he on a team normally?"

"He's excellent...unfortunately," Jacob's words trailed off.

"Did you say he's always on a team opposite Brad?"

"Yeah...they tried them on the same team once...but it was a disaster!"

"What do you mean?" Billy rubbed his chin.

Jacob didn't look away from the teams stepping up: a mixture of all year groups so far, including Skylar from their year and House. Jacob whistled and cheered her on before answering, "Freddie didn't really act like they were on the same side, kept "accidentally"," Jacob made air quotations with his fingers when he said 'accidentally', "hitting him with the ball and chain." He cheered again as a tall thin black girl stepped up and pulled on a yellow bib.

"Who's that?"

Jacob stood tall and a proud, wide smile spread from ear to ear, "That's Priscilla, my big sister! She's year eleven." Billy noticed the rubber dagger by her side. She had thick, tight curls. Half her head of hair was dyed blue. She smiled at the crowd, her teeth beautifully white and straight. Billy could see the family similarity now, although her height should have been a give away that they were related.

In the next few minutes all positions on the teams were filled. Brad was in the centre ready for kick off, Skylar was on a wing and so was Priscilla. Opposite Brad in the centre was a growling Freddie. The pair were both muscular, and in the centre circle looked more like they were about to wrestle, not play a football game.

Mr Leadbetter stood to the side of the pitch ready to referee. "Isn't he supposed to be on the pitch to referee?" asked Billy.

"Are you crazy? He doesn't want to get in the way of the game...especially if Freddie's playing!"

They watched as Mr Leadbetter placed the whistle to his lips. Jacob added, "Plus, apart from the ball, pitch layout and goals, it's not really played the same as English football, is it?" The whistle pierced through the air.

"I guess not," said Billy, his words lost to the roar of the crowd.

Brad kicked the ball away to Priscilla, who flung it to someone else that Billy never knew, a boy with green hair hanging round his shoulders. He missed it and a girl in a green tunic and a red bib blocked it with her rubber sword.

"Isn't that hand ball?" protested Billy.

"Nope! Didn't touch it with her hand, did she?"

The ball dropped to her feet and she booted towards the goal. Skylar tried to intercept it but was pushed aside by a red-bibbed boy. She fell into the water, and the game continued as she flailed around waving her arms and bobbing up and down.

The boy laughed at her and kicked the ball sending it closer to the goal. A blue-tipped arrow whooshed through the air colliding with the ball and knocking it off course. The arrow dropped and floated on the surface of the water.

A boy from Air House in a yellow bib cleared the ball to the other end of the pitch, where Brad headered the ball past a stunned goalkeeper. Brad dived into the water as he followed the header through. He rose back up as a Hammerhead shark, bursting through the water's surface just as Mr Leadbetter blew the whistle for a change of teams.

Brad summersaulted and rolled across the grass. He smiled widely at Freddie, who stomped off of the pitch throwing the red bib at someone waiting to play.

As Billy looked, it was Jake, who was now putting on the bib. Priscilla handed her yellow bib to Jacob. He hugged his sister before realising what he was doing in public and backed off with the bib.

Brad made his way off the pitch scanning the crowd, until his eyes settled on someone and he took very deliberate steps. He handed over the bib, "Show them what you're made of Billy!" He ruffled Billy's hair, again.

"Wait!" he called after Brad.

He turned, "Yes?"

"You fully-manifested in there into a full Hammerhead shark, are we allowed to?"

"There's not really many things not allowed on the pitch, Billy, just try not to kill anyone...that's definitely frowned upon." He half smiled and winked, before turning Billy towards the pitch and pushing him forward. "Just do what comes naturally and you'll be fine, I'm sure, I just have a feeling."

Billy's current natural feeling was nervous and he had a lot of it. His stomach was starting to rumble too since he pretty much skipped breakfast.

He looked over to Jacob, who was arguing with some other boy older than him about being in goal. Eventually,

Jacob won. Two children a lot older than him took centre spot; one dressed in green and the other in white.

Billy had barely stepped onto the pitch before the whistle blew and the field was in motion. The ball flew back and forth, and within a minute the first goal was scored. Jacob rubbed the back of his neck mumbling to himself about letting a goal in; a goal scored by Jake no less. No-one had manifested or used a weapon and somehow the red team was already winning.

Jacob blasted the ball straight down the other end of the pitch. It bounced off the goalie's hands as he dived for it and both goalie and ball ended up in the water, which made Jacob feel better.

A girl in a red bib made her way towards the ball but took too long to workout what to do. Billy took aim and fired an arrow at her torso knocking her into the water too. She could do nothing but flap her arms as her white tunic soaked up water. Billy fully-manifested and plopped into the water, he burst through the surface of the water, semi-manifested underneath the ball, which flew up into the air and he flung it into the back of the net with a webbed foot, past a semi-manifested Jake, hanging upside down from the cross bar. The whistle blew and the crowd roared in excitement. Billy felt exhilarated.

The teams switched over and Billy sat with Jacob and Malyssa to watch the rest of the try-outs.

The games broke for lunch.

"Mr Leadbetter's still limping," stated Malyssa pointing at him, "I need to help him," she stressed at the boys.

"He said 'no', Malyssa. What can you do?"

She thought deeply for a moment, "We could make a deal...make sure he knows we don't need him to tell us what happened."

"It's worth a shot," said Billy. Jacob was sulking quietly still.

The three of them raced up to Mr Leadbetter to put the idea to him. He had other ideas. As soon as he saw Billy he patted him on the back several times harder than Billy would have liked, congratulating him.

Malyssa looked at Billy and nodded her head at Mr Leadbetter. But, Billy didn't get the message; he just stood there as Mr Leadbetter talked about how well he had done.

"Fine," said Malyssa.

"Fine, what?" asked Mr Leadbetter confused.

"Um...nothing...never mind," Malyssa brushed the hair out of her face with her fingers before proceeding with the plan herself. "Sir, you're hurt and -"

"Not this again! I told you it's just a simple football injury and -"

Malyssa cut him off to Billy and Jacob's shock and awe, "No, it's not, Sir! I saw the blood that seeped through your trouser leg last time."

Mr Leadbetter tried to walk away, but Malyssa called after him, "Sir, we don't need to know how you did it, we just want to help."

He turned and looked at them each in turn, before throwing his arms up into the air, "Fine."

"Great! Roll your trouser leg up." She left off the 'Sir' this time, noted Billy. She was now in charge, he thought and smirked.

Malyssa placed her hand over the gash, which was deep. It was trying to scab, but failing miserably. As she looked at it she could see it was slightly infected.

"We caught you just in time, any longer and you'd start to feel the consequences of that infection in the rest of your body." She kept her hands over the wound. She said nothing.

The two boys and Mr Leadbetter watched in astonishment as the yellow infection faded, the gash sealed over and the leg had a light pink scar.

"Sorry, I can't remove the scar, Sir, you had a deep

cut."

"That's quite alright," said Mr Leadbetter, rolling his trouser leg back down and shaking it testing for pain.

Satisfied he thanked her, "You have quite a gift there, Malyssa. I've not seen it as controlled as that in a child before."

Malyssa blushed and tucked her hair behind her ears. He walked away towards the Round Hall with a spring in his step.

"Looks like you two are both having good days," said Jacob, a touch of bitterness in his tone.

Billy and Malyssa both decided not to respond to his moping and simply dragged him to the cafeteria in the Round Hall.

Billy checked his watch. He still had plenty of time for lunch. "Guys, you go on ahead, I want to go see Miss Leadbetter."

"Why?"

"That glass bowl on my side...I still don't know what it's for. She should be free now." He walked away from the doors towards the main part of the building. The wooden boards creaked ever so slightly under his feet, normally not heard between lessons when it's busy. He took in the fresh smell of wood again, not always could it be appreciated among the many bodies in the school and the smells they give off...some more fragrant than others.

He was about to round the corner to approach Miss Leadbetter's office, until he heard his name mentioned.

Billy recognised the voice to belong to Mr Grasp. He leaned towards the corner trying his best to keep out of sight.

Mr Grasp was talking to Miss Leadbetter. The conversation seemed tense or at least on Mr Grasp's part. He may have been talking quietly, but he was gruff. Miss Leadbetter spoke calmly the whole time.

Billy strained his ear to hear why they were talking about him and why Mr Grasp was so annoyed.

"He should be in Air House, our House!" stated Mr Grasp firmly.

"Firstly, I believe he is in the correct House," responded Miss Leadbetter, "Secondly, he has not shown any sign of a winged Manifestus -"

Mr Grasp cut her off, "But you know he will!"

"This conversation is going round in circles."

Mr Grasp ignored her last comment intent on getting his way, "He could be so powerful. Don't you want him in *our* House?" He raised his voice slightly.

"I would, of course find great pleasure in Billy Wortol

being in Air House. He is, as you stated earlier, very talented and probably will be powerful, but maybe not in the way you think."

"But -"

"The answer is 'no', Mr Grasp," her words were firm but calm.

Mr Grasp's voice turned to a low growl, "I wish your brother was still alive! He knew how to run this academy properly! But, instead, he saved you and the rest of us get to watch you run this place into the ground."

Billy gasped. He slapped a hand to his mouth hoping he wasn't too loud.

Miss Leadbetter remained calm. "Mr Grasp, you may think that fear creates powerful warriors, but I know that love conquers all fear, and therefore creates the best warriors. I will continue to follow the Artist's way."

Warriors? They hadn't mentioned 'warriors' much before, thought Billy. *We're just students...just kids.* He thought the warrior thing must just be a name for those gifted.

Mr Grasp growled and Billy heard footsteps pounding the floorboards coming his way.

"This isn't over, Headmistress!" cried Mr Grasp bitterly.

Billy tip-toed back a bit, quietly, before walking

forward at a normal pace, to give the impression of having just got there. Passing Mr Grasp at the corner he said, "Hello, Sir," in his most pleasant voice.

Mr Grasp kept walking, head down, "Hello, Wortol," he mumbled.

"Ah, Billy, are your ears burning?" Miss Leadbetter smiled warmly at him as if the previous conversation hadn't even taken place.

"Sorry, Miss?"

"Never mind, it's just a saying to mean we were just talking about you."

"Oh, were you? What about me?" said Billy with mock interest. He knew full well what was said.

"That you are a very talented boy, Billy."

It may not have been the whole truth, but it was partly true, they had been talking about his talent, thought Billy.

"Anyway, did you want something?"

"Um, yes," he tilted his head and furrowed his brow trying to remember what it was he'd gone to her for. "Oh, yes, I remember now: I have an empty glass bowl with mesh on it, but it remains empty, and no-one can tell me what it's for, because they don't have one."

She peered off into the distance. "I knew your parents, Billy. If you are anything like them, I expect great things.

I will give you a frog and I want you to study it and when you fully and semi-manifest, copy the moves. Study everything you can about it. Never forget who you are."

"When will I get it?"

Miss Leadbetter placed a hand gently on his shoulder, "I will have it in there by the end of the day."

Billy scrunched up his face, "But, you're in Air House, you're not allowed in our dormitory, so -"

She cut him off knowing where his sentence was going, "That may be, but I'm also Headmistress, and I have free reign around the academy." She smiled softly, a deep contrast to her sharp appearance. Billy glanced at her white and silver spikes. She tilted to one side and Billy caught sight of a partial tattoo. She rolled her shoulders and the tattoo was covered. "Run along to lunch, Billy. I promise it will be there later."

Billy, turned on his heels. "I'd run if I were you, Billy, time is getting on." Billy ran to the Round Hall. He told Jacob the story and then repeated it all to Malyssa after lunch.

Chapter Twelve
Weather Warpers

On Saturday morning, Billy sat opposite Jacob at a round table in the Round Hall for breakfast. Billy watched as Jacob leant sulking on one elbow and pushed his scrambled egg around his plate.

"What's wrong, Jacob? Breakfast, lunch and dinner are your favourite classes!" said Billy, a broad smirk on his face.

"Ha-ha!" said Jacob still sulking and giving Billy a sarcastic smile.

Miss Leadbetter tapped the side of a glass gauntlet brimming with steaming coffee. Despite the quiet sound of the tap, it only took five taps before the Round Hall fell silent. "Boys and girls, on the door of Mr Leadbetter's office you will find pinned the names of the students that have made the two academy teams." She paused, "Mmm, I suggest that you don't all go look at once." Then she went back to her toast and the hall erupted in noise once more. Every student, including those who didn't even try-out for the teams rushed from the hall in a stampede.

In the corridors Billy was pressed against the rough wooden walls, and his cardigan snagged on nail heads sticking out of boards.

Billy ducked and dived under arms and squeezed his way to Mr Leadbetter's office. There, hanging on the door by a nail, were the two sheets of discoloured paper. He ran his eyes over list two, which was closest to him. He reached the bottom and breathed a sigh of relief when he saw Jake Fester's name on the list, but his wasn't.

He strained his gaze to the Woodland Warriors' list: Bradley Jonas was top of the list, 'Captain' written beside his name. Billy could hear the Year Thirteens roaring with pleasure. Violet Bloom was second on the list, then Peter Becker, (a cousin of Jacob's, if Billy remembered correctly).

Billy gasped. Fourth on the list he read: William

Wortol. His heart leapt for joy. He looked to Jacob, with joy spread across his face. Jacob scowled back at him and barged his way back through the crowd. Billy scanned the rest of the team list...Jacob's name wasn't on it.

"Jacob, wait!" Billy called after him, but Jacob continued to storm off until he was back at his table and angrily shoved his cold breakfast into his mouth.

As Billy stepped into the hall he felt Jacob's anger burrowing into his body. He shuffled towards his seat opposite Jacob, keeping his head down, not wanting to see Jacob's frowning face.

"You annoyed with me?" asked Billy, still not looking up.

"What you think?" growled Jacob, stabbing a mushroom.

"Why are you so annoyed? I've not done anything."

"I did nothing but encourage you and look, you made the team! If you'd have done the same to me, we both could have been on the team!"

"I did encourage you -"

Jacob interrupted, "No, you didn't! You consoled me after I failed...just like you're doing now!"

He picked up his tray of unfinished food, moved away and slammed his tray down on a different table.

Jacob avoided Billy all week. Billy had bigger problems: his first football match playing for the Woodland Warriors. He wasn't even sure he wanted to play anymore.

Saturday evening, before bed, Billy approached Brad in the lounge of the Common Room whilst he was chilling in front of the fire with his friends.

"Um, Bradley, can I speak to you?" Billy avoided looking him in the face.

"Call me Brad. Go ahead, Billy."

"No, I mean in private."

The group fell quiet, "Oh yeah, sure, Billy." Brad stood to his feet and gently guided him over to empty seats by the window with blue drawn curtains. The rocking motion of the chairs soothed Billy.

"What's the problem?"

"Um...I'm not sure I want to be on the team." Billy twiddled his thumbs in his lap.

"Is this to do with Jacob?"

"You know?" Billy finally looked up at Brad.

"Yeah, you can't miss the looks he gives you, and he's been talking to Peter about it."

"So, you know why I have to quit then. I'll play this match though."

"Billy, I don't mind if it's your choice to quit the team, we all make our own choices in life, but if you think this is what it takes to keep a friend, it will only end in resentment and bitterness." He stood to his feet and ruffled Billy's hair (he had a habit of doing that). "Think on it," he said, and walked away. He paused and turned back, "And Billy, if he's really your friend he'll be pleased for you; not jealous."

"He said I never encouraged him. I feel bad."

"Well, if that's true, you can change that from now on, but is quitting the team the way to do it?"

Billy breathed in deeply before responding, "But I want to be his friend and this sacrifice will show him, won't it?"

Brad smiled warmly; his green eyes twinkled under the fairy lights covering the Common Room ceiling.

"Will it?" Brad walked away again. He called over his shoulder, "I'd go to bed and get some rest if I was you, first match tomorrow, and you'll need your strength and a sharp mind. Your kit will be upstairs in the morning."

Billy took himself up the twirling staircase to sleep.

Billy stepped onto the pitch with his ten other team Mates. He was the shortest and youngest on the team.

The pitch was encased in stadium seats filled with roaring students and staff, waving flags of two different styles. Most matched his own kit, which was a mix of blue, green and white. He wore brown leather trousers with stitched in padding in the shins. *They were fun to get on for the first time!* His blue football boots laced up over his ankles and partway up his calf. A cotton tunic flowed out and down the back of his thighs. The loose sleeves waved in the wind but were fixed in place by thumbholes. The hood hung about his shoulders and the tunic gathered by cords around his neck. His breastplate armour made of dark blue, green and white leathers hugged his torso. A helmet, made similarly, squeezed his head. Billy found it incredibly uncomfortable, but apparently it was necessary, according to Brad. He had seen a professional footballer lose an ear!

The Mighty Manifestums marched in unison onto the pitch. Each one scowling and wearing an all black kit, with all the same pieces as the Woodland Warriors.

Brad had explained at breakfast that the teams were named by the original team captains of The Gifted Academy hundreds of years ago. The captain of Mighty Manifestums prided himself on the gifts those in the realm had and the captain of Woodland Warriors prided his team on the calling to protect; not the gift alone. He told Billy that The Beast is said to be the original captain of Mighty Manifestums, attaching himself in spirit form to other Manifestums so that he never dies.

Billy was learning more and more about The Beast, and every piece of information was worse than the last. The Beast could be anyone at this rate.

The two teams spread out over the pitch. Bradley Jonas stood in the centre circle opposite Damien Crusher. Mr Leadbetter's whistle screeched and the ball was in play.

Billy had never seen so many people manifest at the same time. It got quite confusing remembering who was who when they were manifested.

Billy hardly touched the ball in the first half. In fact, the only times he touched it was when he didn't dodge it in time and he was battered across the pitch. There was more land fortunately due to the bigger size of the pitch, so most of the time he could quickly get back to his feet.

The whistle blew after an uneventful first half. The supporters of Mighty Manifestums cheered loudly. They were up by two goals.

"Billy, we need you out there," said a desperate Brad. He handed a cup of water to Billy. "I know it's a lot to get your head around, but if you can't remember who's on our team, just get the ball towards the opposite goal." He placed his hands on Billy's shoulders, "We can do this."

Billy sat quietly trying to memorise who was which animal. He looked over to the crowds waving flags and yelling. He spotted Jacob at the front without a flag and Malyssa was with him frantically waving her flag for the Woodland Warriors.

Billy looked over to the nearby trees as a sudden raucous of birdcalls sounded over the cries of people and hundreds of birds were flapping above the trees. They soared away to the woods where the cabin was. Billy had read enough books on wildlife to know that the sudden departure of birds meant a change in the weather... *although they did only fly to another woodland area not too far and still on the academy grounds*...But Billy heeded the warning anyway.

Half time break time seemed over quickly, but Billy was pretty certain he knew the animals of the other players on his team.

Once again, when the whistle blew, Damien and Brad were at loggerheads. Brad kicked the ball away and immediately pulled an arrow from his quiver, blasting a member of the other team away from the ball that soared through the air towards Peter. Peter semi-manifested and took flight after the ball kicking it towards Lily, who used her lion speed to dribble it closer to the goal where Brad reappeared having swam through the water as a Hammerhead shark.

Billy still didn't feel like much use. He had to get stuck in. He had to forget about the problem with Jacob. Maybe if he played well Jacob would see he was supposed to be on the team. He looked to see where the ball was as it reached the back of the net. The goal put them only one goal behind Mighty Manifestums. The Woodland Warriors screamed with excitement. "Whoop! Whoop! Woodland Warriors!"

Billy focused his eyes on the ball. He felt the first splurges of rain on his face. They were big splurges too. He saw the ball dip over the middle of the water and he manifested diving in after it as the rain continued to get heavier and heavier and the sky grew blacker and blacker.

On the surface the players and spectators found it hard to see. The wind whipped their faces and rain ran from their hair into their eyes.

"Look!" yelled Malyssa banging on Jacob's arm.

"What?"

"The water! There're great big waves! Billy's going to get hurt! He's going to drown! We have to do something!"

"We can't do anything, we're not allowed on the pitch."

"Look over there!" she pointed not too far into the distance at blue skies and sunshine. "This makes no sense, the storm is just over the pitch."

"Could be a Weather Warper!" cried Jacob above the storm.

"You're right, Jacob! But, who here has that skill?" she squinted looking at everybody suspiciously.

Chelsea Grease scowled up at the sky from the pitch waving her arms around. "There, Jacob! It's Chelsea!"

The wind became so strong it lifted the goal posts and the players could do nothing. The ball had blown off the pitch. Mr Leadbetter blew the whistle for a time-out. It could barely be heard. The spectators were ushered away from the stadium.

Brad was getting his team away from the pitch. He reached Violet, but she wouldn't budge. "He's still in there, Brad! We can't leave him! He's one of us!"

"I'm ordering you to leave the - "

But before he could finish his sentence, Violet was in

the water. She manifested into an Octopus before disappearing beneath the waves. Minutes, which felt like hours, passed before she appeared again, gasping for breath and being forced back under water by wave after wave.

She eventually made her way to the edge, dragging an unconscious Billy behind her. Brad and Mr Leadbetter pulled them both out of the water and away from the pitch.

Miss Leadbetter worked on reversing the storm elements.

Billy was none the wiser. In his unconscious state he was back in the other realm, where his mother and sister remained. He saw The Beast all over the television screens of stores. He saw those from the mystical realm walking around semi-manifested evoking fear from the ones they should have been protecting. The sky was grey. Billy looked at his own clothes. They were tatty and torn, so much worse than reality. He saw Jess. He called to her, "Jess! Jess!" She looked at him but didn't move. Her hair was tangled and her dress ripped. Then he noticed the chain around her neck attached to a smartly dressed semi-manifested woman. Her wings stretched wide like a dragon. He screamed out for his sister one last time,

"Jess!"

He woke suddenly, mumbling her name as he tossed his head from side to side by the edge of the pitch. The rain had stopped.

"You gave us a scare, Billy," said Miss Leadbetter.

"I-I saw Jess, she - "

"She is fine, Billy, you've been out cold for a while. You are to spend the rest of the day resting."

"Who won?"

"Mighty Manifestum, but it wasn't a full game."

Billy closed his eyes.

"You seem to be getting yourself into a lot of dangerous circumstances, Billy. I wonder why." She winked at him.

He had no idea why. The circumstances happened to him; they weren't his choice.

"Go back to your dormitory when you're ready. I'll get someone to keep an eye on you." She helped him to his feet. "Brad, take him back and ask a friend of his to watch him." Turning back to Billy, she said, "I do *not* want to see you before dinner this evening, understood?"

Billy nodded and let Brad lead him to the dormitories. Once there he ordered Jacob to look after Billy, "Make sure he doesn't sleep." Jacob merely nodded.

PART THREE
THE FIGHTING

Chapter Thirteen
Duels and Distractions

Billy sat up in bed leaning on his headboard trying to keep his eyes open. Jacob was doing the exact same thing on his own bed next to him. Both wondered who would speak first and what to say.

Finally, Billy spoke, "Sorry."

Jacob turned to stare at him, and Billy could feel his eyes on him and thought he had just opened a can of worms. But to his surprise, Jacob merely asked, "What for?"

"For getting on to the team when - "

"No, no, Billy, I didn't literally mean for you to tell me the things you're sorry for, I meant: you have nothing to be sorry for."

Billy looked at Jacob, who was looking sheepishly at his sleeping bag following a line of stitching with his finger.

As if knowing Billy was looking at him for answers Jacob continued, "I was being a bit of a baby about not making the team."

"But, you said I hadn't encouraged you, so I'm sorry for that," said Billy.

"You had encouraged me...I was just blaming you because I was disappointed with myself. I'd been bragging to everyone how I was going to make the team and was embarrassed, so...I guess...I blamed you." He looked up at Billy waiting for a response to his honesty.

"Thanks. Well, I'm still sorry for..." said Billy. He searched the room with his eyes for an idea, and saw a pair of football boots muddied on the wooden flooring, "...for losing the game today."

"You didn't lose the game. It wasn't your fault."

"I wasn't very good, though."

"Maybe...but, you nearly died, so all is forgiven, Mate." He smirked at Billy, who laughed at his friend's logic.

Billy suddenly felt the sharp pain on the back of his head, "Ow!" He raised a hand to it and could feel the egg-shaped bump through his thick hair. "What happened to me anyway?"

Jacob rubbed his own head mirroring Billy, "Well, you were in the water, manifested and a huge storm came and you were knocked against a rock or something, but Violet Bloom saved you!"

"I was knocked out in a storm? But everyone else seems OK," stated Billy. He was forlorn at the realisation he was yet again the only one to be hurt.

"Yeah, but Mate, no-one else was in the water with the huge crashing waves! They were nearly as big as me!"

Billy looked at the height of Jacob, "Really? You're exaggerating to make me feel better. Aren't you?"

Jacob shook his head and sprung to his feet, "Seriously, Mate, they were up here probably!" Jacob tapped his shoulder.

Billy was still not convinced and raised an eyebrow gently nodding, knowing full well a storm couldn't do that just over a football pitch and destroy nothing else.

Jacob could see that Billy didn't believe him, "It wasn't a normal storm. We reckon it was Chelsea Grease that caused it; me and Malyssa that is!"

"People can't cause storms, Jacob, but thanks."

"Before you came here, you didn't think people could

turn into animals either, did you?"

"Good point," said Billy. "OK, so how did this 'Chelsea' create a storm?"

"She must be a Weather Warper!"

"A what?"

"Seriously? Have you not even flicked through your books?"

Billy looked at him blankly. Jacob rolled his eyes. He rummaged in the bedside cabinet for his Science book. He flicked through until he found 'Weather Warpers' near the back of the book. Billy noticed the book was in alphabetical order, something he'd not noticed during his classes.

Jacob turned the book to face Billy and plonked himself on Billy's bed next to him so he could talk him through it. "So, a Weather Warper can manipulate the weather, so it's not magic, they work with what's available, bending the laws of nature."

Billy looked at the sketch in the book of a man using his hands to cause a whirlpool in the sea.

"Can everyone do that?" asked Billy.

"Yes and no. We all have the capacity to, because we all have the power inside of us since we are connected to the Artist, but only some nurture or practice it and clearly use it for different things: some to help and some to destroy..."

Billy didn't respond.

"Oh, I don't think Chelsea wanted to destroy you, Billy...probably just scare you and keep you occupied during the game. Think it just got out of hand."

I wouldn't be so sure, thought Billy, *it wouldn't be the first time someone tried to kill me.* He thought back to what he could remember or imagined happened the day his father died saving him from drowning.

Jacob noticed Billy's glassy eyes and slammed the book closed pulling Billy out of his own mind abruptly. "Well, that's enough about that! Let's play some card games until dinner."

"Um...yeah, sure." Billy didn't know many games.

Jacob reached into the draw of his bedside cabinet, and pulled out a bluish-green pack of cards. "Be careful with these, they're my favourite. My family gave me these last Christmas - they're holographic!" He pulled the cards out of the box and placed the box to one side carefully. Billy read the box aloud, "Ocean Giants."

"'Course, it's Ocean Giants! Well...there's all different versions, but this is obviously my favourite!"

Suddenly, a voice came from above them, "Can I

play?" And both Billy and Jacob jumped. The deck of cards scattered on the floor and bed. They looked up to see Lesley hanging over the edge of the ledge of the storage area (or his sleeping area).

"Don't do that again!" shouted Jacob, "get down here if you're going to play!"

Lesley scrambled down the rope ladder and knelt next to Billy's bed.

"What are we playing?"

"Old Maid," replied Jacob removing one of the two Joker cards only.

Billy looked at the moving Joker card lying on his bed.

"Who's that?" he asked looking at the bearded man in the usual jester hat. He wore a red tunic and black leather armour. He had one eye closed and looked like the photo had been taken at the worst possible moment; like a bad yearbook photo that the editor refused to change.

Jacob and Lesley started laughing, "That's the captain of Red Sea Raiders. They're like the unofficial enemies of Ocean Giants. No-one here will support them because they're not a local team!" explained Jacob. "There's another Joker in the pack in yellow; he's the captain of Sandstormers!"

"Nice!" said Lesley, "You've got an excellent pack!"

"Are they not all the same, then?" asked Billy.

"Nope!" said Lesley and Jacob together before Jacob explained that there were hundreds of different options of Jokers and some people would own other team decks and unfortunately an Ocean Giant player could be the Joker in that pack.

Jacob quickly explained the rules of the game. They played until it was time to go to dinner, laughing and giggling the whole time; especially at how often Billy was the 'Old Maid'. He lost a lot. *How did he keep ending up with the Joker in his hand when the game was over?*

In the Round Hall, the cafeteria had once again been set up by the entrance. Billy and Jacob queued for their food with Malyssa, who had met them outside where she had been waiting for them.

Lesley had gone to talk to a couple of his friends from the other Houses.

Whilst they were putting pasta onto their trays, they were knocked sideways by people near them as the voice of Jake could be heard, "Move it! Let us in!" They had obviously barged their way into the line.

"You don't need to push!" shouted Malyssa annoyed that some of her pasta had landed on the floor.

"Keep your nose out, Bug!"

"Don't keep calling her that, like it 's something bad!" ordered Billy.

Jake pushed those in front of him out of the way and squared up to Billy. He was bigger than Billy in every physical way and looked down at Billy past his flat nose that looked like it was pinned back and you could see right up his nostrils, even if you weren't shorter than him like Billy was. "What did you say to me?" He towered over Billy, who stood his ground looking braver than he was feeling.

"You heard me, Jake. There's nothing wrong with being an insect and Malyssa is very skilled."

Malyssa beamed.

"She's definitely got more skill than you, hasn't she Wart?" Jake grinned cruelly. Quinn and Frankie were either side of Jake and grinning the same. "You couldn't even make it through one football match without needing to be rescued. You seem to be getting hurt a lot here, Wart...maybe this realm is telling you that you shouldn't be here!"

Billy said nothing and Jake turned to pile pasta onto his own tray.

"He deserves to be here...more than you do!" blurted

Jacob, taking them all by surprise.

Jake suddenly turned on him. He glared at him trying to intimidate him, like he does others, but Jacob might be gangly, but he was just as tall as Jake and glared straight back.

"Is that so?" Jake got so far in Jacob's face that Jacob started to lean back, so that he didn't breathe in Jake's bad breath.

"Billy's a better player, warrior and Manifestum than you'll ever be!" He stepped back to stand up straight and stare down Jake. "You didn't help your team, you just flew around as a bat avoiding everything! We all saw!"

Jake growled, "Fine! Me and Billy, one on one, midnight at the 5-a-side pitch!" He turned from Jacob to Billy, "Be there! We'll see who's the best!" He walked away followed by his two shadows, Quinn and Frankie.

Malyssa took her food and immediately started telling Jeremy, Blossom and other friends in her House what was happening.

Billy and Jacob went to sit at an empty table. The mutterings about the upcoming duel spread like wild fire around the Round Hall in a matter of minutes.

"Jacob, what have you got me into?"

"It's a duel! Not with pistols and glove slapping,

although it would have been great to see you slap that smug face with a glove. You'll show him that you're better and wipe that smirk off his face!"

"But, I don't care who's better. I just wanted him to stop putting down Malyssa. I certainly didn't want a one-on-one with him, especially not tonight...I'm still recovering from being knocked out." He spooned some twisty pasta into his mouth.

"Oh...now...well...yes, I did forget about that," said Jacob, "Guess I got a bit carried away, didn't I?"

"Well, you can come watch and get me out of there if it gets too much!" Although Billy thought it was more likely 'when' than 'if' it got too much. "Is there anything I should know for tonight?"

"Yeah," replied Jacob, "You play on one side of the pitch shooting at the same goal. You have your weapons. You'll probably be playing by torchlight so that the teachers aren't alerted. And you'll probably get hurt a bit so...um...I'll bring Malyssa with me or tell her to meet us there."

"Great," mumbled Billy leaning on one elbow, not the least bit excited about the match.

After dinner all the students returned to their House Common Rooms. Billy stared at the fireplace, the orange flames flickering, contemplating the night ahead. He had to go to bed like everyone else because it was against academy rules to be out of bed after 'lights out' call. He and Jacob would have to sneak out and hope Malyssa manages to as well. There was only one good thing about the match: at least it would keep him awake and away from his nightmares.

Mr Leadbetter called. "Lights out!" at ten o'clock. Quickly the Common Room emptied as students climbed the swirling staircases.

Billy played on top of his sleeping bag, but after a while he felt his eyes begin to get heavy. He propped himself up. As he went to readjust his pillow to lean back on, he felt something under it. He grabbed the torch from his bedside unit, opened up his sleeping bag and pulled it over him, the torch and the object, like it was tent. The torch lit up the object. It was an envelope with 'Billy' scrawled across it. He turned it over. It wasn't sealed. He quietly unfolded the envelope flap and pulled out the paper. He looked straight at the bottom to see whom it was from. The sender was Brad. Billy read the letter in his head:

Dear Billy,

I've heard, as I'm sure you're aware have most people, about the duel tonight. Be careful, duels can be worse than matches sometimes, remember there's no referee, which means there's no-one to stop rules being broken.

It's obviously going to be dark and Jake's a bat so he'll have exceptional hearing. He's also human and can see, so he has the advantage there, too. But, he's also governed primarily by his mind and he's proud. He will think of ways to fight dirty and you need to rise above that. You have a strong soul being in Water House; don't stoop to his level...no matter what happens. There will always be another way to do things that's fairer and right. Follow the way of the Artist and He will steer you right.

Take your bow and arrows with rubber casings. I can't come help you because too many people down there is bound to draw attention from the teachers.

Remember winning isn't everything.

P.S. Check your bedside draw, I've put something in there. It's the only way I can help.

Yours sincerely,

Brad.

Billy slid open the bedside draw and shone the torch light over the items in there. Sitting on top of a notebook that belonged to him was a torch with an elasticated strap. He pulled it out. After a closer inspection he realised it was a headlamp. *Great idea*, he thought, *I can keep my hands free to use the bow and arrow.* He stretched it onto his head.

At quarter to twelve he woke a snoring Jacob from his slumber. The pair crept quietly down the outside spiral staircase, hoping to be less likely to disturb any sleepers. If they did, the sounds are more likely to be attributed to natural outdoor noise, Billy assumed.

They made their way by Billy's headlamp alone, (as Jacob's torch was pretty useless), to the 5-a-side pitch.

Malyssa was nowhere to be seen. Jake stood alone, his own headlamp shining in Billy's direction. He didn't appear to have brought anyone with him.

"I didn't think you'd show!" he shouted to Billy loud enough for Billy to hear but not to reach the dormitories.

"If you didn't think I'd come, why are you here?" asked Billy. His light lit up the woodlands a little nearby. The creepiness and the chilly night air sent a shudder down his spine.

"Just in case!" snapped back Jake. "Let's start!"

"Wait! Where's the ball?" It wasn't on the centre spot like it was supposed to be.

"Over there!" Jake turned in the direction of the goal.

His headlamp picked up a white sphere on the penalty spot. Jake leapt into the air and semi-manifested, his black wings that resembled dragon wings, spread out. He looked more intimidating than ever in the moonlight.

Billy sprang into action; he set an arrow on his bow and flung it in Jake's direction. It struck his torso with a thud and sent him off course.

Billy wanted to avoid the water in the dark and instead of leaping into the water he bounced on his frog legs around the inside edge of the pitch. He manifested to human legs and booted the ball towards the empty goal, but suddenly Jake swung down fro the cross bar, hanging upside down from it, his large bat wings filling up most of the goal. The ball bounced off his left wing out towards the far corner. Jake fully manifested and flew after it.

Billy was closer to the goal. He leaped towards it; his small frame barely took up any space. Jake had changed back to human form; he dribbled the ball towards Billy with his bow steadied and an arrow pointing at Billy.

Billy quickly pulled an arrow from his quiver and aimed it at Jake. Jake stopped dribbling the ball.

"You're better than I thought, Wart Boy!" Jake smiled. "But I'm better!"

234

There was a sudden howl from Jacob at the edge of the pitch. Billy kept his arrow pointing at Jake, fully tensed, but turned to look at Jacob. Billy's light picked up the edges of two figures pounding their fists into Jacob. Jacob dropped to the ground and curled into a ball as the figures kicked him repeatedly showing no mercy.

Billy looked back at Jake horrified.

"What's it going to be, Wart?"

Billy lowered his arrow. He contemplated removing the rubber tip and shooting Jake, but that wasn't right.

Jake cackled. Billy raised his bow once again.

"Oh, now that I wasn't expecting! Maybe old Grasp is right about you after all! You have got Air qualities in you!"

Suddenly, Billy turned his bow towards one of the figures; he let the arrow fly. It caught one in his unarmoured back and sent him sprawling. Billy started running towards the one figure left towering over Jacob, whilst reloading an arrow. He drew it back and released it. It flew through the air taking out the other figure. Both figures scrambled to their feet and made a run for it.

"Jacob! Jacob! Are you OK?" Billy knelt beside him trying to see him by torchlight. Malyssa came running out of the shadows she had been hiding in.

She looked at the blood trickling from Jacob's nose and lip. There were other cuts and bruises she couldn't see, but she could sense them. A tear rolled down her cheek.

"Wart Boy!" Jake called grabbing Billy's attention. Billy looked up just in time to see the ball soar into the back of the net, before Jake manifested and flew away towards the dormitories.

Billy turned his attention back to Jacob, who still said nothing. Malyssa placed her hands on Jacob's cheeks. The bleeding stopped and dried. Jacob's eyes blinked open and he groaned. Billy let out an audible sigh of relief and hugged Jacob who winced in pain still.

Chapter Fourteen
Harvest Festival

It was the 5th of November. Billy joined Jacob and Malyssa by the little pond he had discovered in the woods in the first week at the academy. It was secluded most of the time.

Billy turned the collar up on his navy blue suede jacket to protect him from the autumnal chill. The collar and cuffs were a lighter blue than the rest. The academy sure seemed to like their House colours.

The new season changed the appearance of the woodland. Already, yellowing leaves clung to twigs and the deep green of evergreen conifers mingled in with the bronzing woodlands. Soft golden slanted rays of sun reached farther into the wood than when he had first seen this spot a couple of months earlier.

The low sun shone through the beech trees creating a serene scene, and picked up the copper tones of the fallen leaves that created a thick carpet. The sound of barking deer in the distance added to the beauty of the season.

That night they would celebrate it in all its glory. Thanking the Artist for the change of seasons and the coming harvests. Billy didn't really know the Artist well. He had heard many stories of the creator of the realms and somewhere in the deepest part of his mind he thought he knew more that hadn't been told to him. *But how could that possibly be when he hadn't heard of this place until earlier that year? With the way his mind worked he thought Miss Leadbetter was definitely right: he shouldn't be in Air House!*

The celebrations coincided with England's 'Bonfire Night' so that families in the Humanum world could celebrate to their hearts' content without drawing attention to themselves. Fireworks with the bright colours exploding all over the night skies were obviously a hard thing to keep under wraps.

Billy had already seen the decorating team weaving more fairy light s throughout the woods and a track leading to the main part of the academy. There were none in this patch of the woods.

Malyssa's stone landed in the pond with a 'plop'.

"Finally, you're here!" stated Jacob, "We've been waiting here for ages! We were beginning to think you weren't coming!"

Billy rammed his cold hands into his coat pockets and hunched his shoulders. Malyssa and Jacob seemed to be nice and warm in their suede coats. Jacob's was another faded second-hand coat and Malyssa's white one with silver collar and cuffs was so big and new it swamped her like a big white yeti.

"So, what is so secretive you couldn't tell us anywhere but here?" asked Malyssa. She blew on her hands and rubbed them together.

"You're sure we're alone?" asked Billy.

"Pretty sure, yes," replied Jacob, "I don't see or hear anyone...do you?"

"No. OK." Billy huddled them together and spoke softly. "I didn't tell you something I witnessed a while back between Miss Leadbetter and Mr Grasp."

"Why?" asked Jacob, "Don't you trust us?"

"That wasn't the reason. It was just a lot to take in and a lot has been happening, but I want to find out more."

They stared at him in anticipation, "Well, go on then," said Malyssa.

"It's about the Leadbetter's brother, Brutus. He used to be Headmaster here."

"We know, it's in the History books," stated Jacob.

"He's the one who was supposed to have died saving Miss Leadbetter."

"Again, we know, Billy. I couldn't remember the name before, but I remembered a short while after we saw him in the cabin," said Malyssa.

"Why didn't you say anything?" asked Billy.

"Same reason as you: I've been processing the information," replied Malyssa.

"Does it not bother you that not only is he alive, but he's joined The Beast?"

"Yes, of course, Mate."

"I've been wondering what could make a good guy turn bad, since we found out the truth about him," said Malyssa. She sighed. "But I can't work it out."

"But that's what I wanted to say: what about if he didn't turn bad?"

"You mean he's still good?" asked Jacob pressing his lips into a fine line.

"No - "

"Good, because the Brutus we saw is definitely not a good guy!" Jacob raised his eyebrows seeking agreement.

"Let me finish," said Billy, "What if he's always been bad?"

"But he saved Miss Leadbetter," said Malyssa.

"Maybe, but we've already discovered part of the story isn't true, maybe the rest isn't either."

"They're pretty big differences and accusations, Billy," said Jacob.

"OK, let me tell you what I heard," said Billy. "Mr Grasp was talking about wanting me in Air House and Miss Leadbetter was adamant that it wasn't happening. He then got really cross saying she should have died that day; not her brother."

Malyssa gasped and covered her mouth, "How could he say that?"

"Miss Leadbetter didn't seem too bothered by it. Anyway, he also said that she was running the academy into the ground and that Brutus had known how to be a powerful leader by making people fear him." He paused and looked at each of them in the eyes before continuing, "Does that sound like a good guy?"

"No...not really. And we know that Mr Grasp thought The Beast's power was a good thing, so...I guess, you *could* be right," said Malyssa, tucking hair behind her ears and glasses.

"I want to find out more about him," said Billy.

"How are you going to do that?" asked Jacob.

"I'm going back to the cabin tonight!"

Malyssa and Jacob shook their heads in despair. "You can't go back!" stated Malyssa.

"I can and I will! I have to! There's more to this, Malyssa!"

Malyssa threw her arms in the air defeated, "Fine, but you can't go alone."

"Yes, Malyssa's right, we're coming too!"

"You can't, I need you to cover for me."

"To who?"

"Whoever asks. I'm sure Mr Leadbetter will disappear during the Harvest Festival tonight like he does every evening. I'm going to follow him. If anyone sees I'm not there, I need you to make up something. If all three of us are missing they might suspect we're up to something, especially that Mr Grasp!"

"Fine! But just this once, you hear me! We do the rest together! And we want to hear what you learn!" commanded Malyssa, arms folded and her foot tapping on the leaves.

"Deal! Thanks!" Billy hugged them both; "I suppose we should go up to the Round Hall for dinner and celebrations.

When Billy stepped through the glass doors to the Round Hall he was gobsmacked. It looked amazing! Completely transformed! There was still the same circular layout, and the guardians were still lining the walls, *why did he only see them in the hall and nowhere else?* But, from the centre of the ceiling strings of lights twinkled to the walls like thousands of fireflies. They wound round the beams.

The main lights were out. Candles in jars of various sizes lit tables. Hay bales were placed around the hall.

Around the teachers' table were displayed various foods like pumpkins, onions, potatoes, carrots and many other vegetables.

With the candles and lights alone, the hall had a mystical atmosphere, but through the strings of lights the decorating team had woven vines of leaves made of fabric in oranges, reds, yellows and browns. They twisted them round the tables and chairs too.

The food being served added to the warmth of the room: jacket potatoes and a vegetable chilli. Beautiful apples dripping with toffee stood on a tray upside down;

ready to be devoured for dessert.

And what Billy liked the most, which he thought was an extra touch that just topped off the evening, was the orange coloured hot chocolate. It looked wonderful served in their glass mugs, which were wider at the top and narrowed to a little decorative stem joining it to the base. The glass was finished with a glass handle. Billy filled his mug to the brim and squirted cream on top and finished it with a dusting of chocolate powder.

Once everyone was seated, once again Miss Leadbetter tapped her own glass mug until there was silence in the hall. "Today, we celebrate another year of agricultural provision. The crops have delivered us delicious food. We should be thankful for our nourishing creations! This evening we will celebrate our gratitude to the Artist! Continue!" The Round Hall once again filled with the sound of clinking mugs, cutlery on plates and the students talking simultaneously.

"I thought this was a party," said Billy.

"It is, once dinner is over we can move around and dance to music played by The Gifted Academy band."

"Oh, that's probably the best time to slip off. Let's keep an eye on Mr Leadbetter. It was long after the violins, guitars and drums started that Billy saw Mr

Leadbetter exchange glances with his sister and slip out of the hall. Billy followed him. He knew where he was going so it didn't matter if he lost him as long as he witnessed him talk with Brutus.

Billy exited from the wooden building, the cool November hit him and made him shiver. He tried not to tense up and trap the cold in his muscles. It wasn't easy.

On the steps he was well lit by fairy lights. He quickly dashed into the nearest group of trees. They were still lit up, but at least he could hide behind them if need be.

Leaves crunched under his feet no matted how softly he stepped. He was grateful when he reached the edge of the 5-a-side football pitch. He let his eyes adjust to the darkness beyond the woods before carefully making his way across the centre of the pitch, across the remaining field and into the woodlands surrounding the cabin. He was terrified every step of the way.

He reached the barbed wire fence; diligently sneezed between two wires without snagging his clothes and crouched over by the same window as before, which was well illuminated by the light of the fire in the hearth.

He liked that they were less likely to see him in the dark, especially as the inside was lit, they would likely just see their reflections.

Billy watched Mr Leadbetter stirring something. It looked like muddy water.

"It's that time of day, Brutus. Open wide!" Brutus groaned as Mr Leadbetter held his nose forcing him to open his mouth, into which he poured the muddy liquid.

Billy watched as Brutus was forced to swallow the liquid. Brutus wretched when Mr Leadbetter stepped away.

"You can't give me that stuff forever!" growled Brutus at his brother.

"Why not? I grow the ingredients myself!" Mr Leadbetter strutted to the sink and hummed as he rinsed the cup out.

"You're a disgrace to the Manifestums! Making me no-more than a Humanum! Don't you remember what happened the last time you tried your concoction out on people, to prevent manifesting?" He grinned baring yellow teeth.

Mr Leadbetter turned suddenly towards him, "Shut up!" he yelled.

"That's right, you do remember, don't you?"

Mr Leadbetter flew at Brutus, grabbing him by the scruff of his jacket.

Brutus laughed maniacally.

"Shut up!" screamed Mr Leadbetter, shaking his brother. Brutus stopped laughing. Mr Leadbetter stepped back and swept a hand over his blue mohican, trying to collect himself.

"Yep, you're not the blue-eyed boy everyone thinks you are, are you Jez?"

Mr Leadbetter glared at him, a look of fear in his eyes. "I said shut up," he said between gritted teeth.

"You could always kill, brother. It wouldn't be the first time you killed someone would it now?" He raised an eyebrow, "Shall I remind us of what happened?"

Mr Leadbetter didn't respond, he simply paced the room, wondering what to do.

"You used to try this concoction on our parents. Do you remember giving it to them on the day of the fire?" He looked at Mr Leadbetter's white face, "You do, don't you?" He chuckled. "They had no idea you were secretly testing your potions on them, did they?"

Mr Leadbetter refused to speak.

"They had no chance in the fire. They couldn't manifest. They were stuck like mere Humanums as the flames licked at their bodies, burning them alive." He licked his lips. "Does our dear old sister know it's your fault they died that day? That because of you they couldn't escape?" His eyes sparkled with the flickering of the flames from the cabin's hearth. "You killed them, Jez!"

"Shut up! No more!" Mr Leadbetter had tears streaming down his face.

"Unfortunately, in a moment of weakness, I helped our sister escape, but I've got stronger since! And it won't happen again!"

Mr Leadbetter dropped to his knees, covering his face with his hands.

"How would our dear sister feel knowing that you started the fire with one of your stupid Bunsen burners?" He cackled with glee. "And how does it feel for you to now learn that the fire you started, which killed our parents was also the distraction that paved the way for The Beast to storm through the realm?"

Mr Leadbetter sobbed and pleaded him to stop.

But he didn't. "And you still continue to make and use this concoction of yours! You're disgusting!"

Billy could barely breathe on the other side of the cabin wall. He leant against the rotting wood and inhaled deep breaths before running like his life depended on it. The tree branches whipped him in the face and caught his hair, but he didn't care, he just wanted to be back with his friends and well away from both Mr Leadbetters.

Back at the Round Hall, the jovial music still played. He shook the leaves from his hair before he ran into the hall. He searched like a mad man until he found Jacob and Malyssa laughing over more hot chocolate as they sat on a hay bale. He ran to them and launched himself at them hugging them tightly.

"Hey! You're spilling my hot chocolate, Mate! What's wrong?" asked Jacob, wiping the liquid off his cardigan as best he could with his hand.

Billy said nothing; he just squeezed them tighter.

"Billy? Talk to us. Come sit down." Malyssa separated herself from him and budged up so that he could sit between her and Jacob.

Eventually, he was calm enough that he was able to share everything that happened. The three of them sat in deep discussion for the rest of the celebration.

When the festivities drew to a close, all the students, except the decorating team and band, made their way to the glass doors to leave. It was a horrible bottleneck.

Billy was not far past the teachers' table when he felt a tap on his shoulder. He turned to see, to his surprise, Miss Leadbetter. She smiled sweetly at him. Somehow, he felt calmer looking at the twinkle in her eyes from the fairy lights hanging above.

"Step over to the teachers' table, I want to speak with you."

Billy followed her as Jacob and Malyssa continued to the doors unaware he had left them.

"How are you getting on studying the frog I gave you?"

"Um...to be honest, not great. The main thing I learned is how much noise they can make." He shuffled on the spot feeling awkward.

Miss Leadbetter laughed. "Yes, they can be noisy, with all the croaking or belching," she said, "Well, keep at it, I'm sure you will notice some fascinating and useful things to improve your performance."

"I will, Miss Leadbetter." He turned to walk away.

"Billy, I wasn't finished. That was just a catch up," she called after him.

"Oh, sorry." He pivoted and stood in front of her once more.

"Wait here," she directed him.

Billy stayed where he was and watched her climb the steps to her own table and briefly duck out of sight. She reappeared with a small leather-bound book. She descended the stairs, went back to her position in front of him and held the book out to him. Billy just looked at it.

"Take it, then," she shook it at him.

Billy gingerly took hold of it. He turned it around in his hands. The book was well-worn and the pages were dog-eared.

"Thank you," he said, "But...what is it?"

"That," she pointed at the book, "Is everything I have found out so far about crows."

Billy looked at her and gulped. *Did she, too, believe he would manifest as a crow?*

"Know your enemy, Billy," she said with a smile. Then she walked away, without even giving him the opportunity to ask why she was giving the book to him and no-one else.

He fell asleep that night flicking through the book by torchlight under his sleeping bag.

Chapter Fifteen
A Family Christmas

Billy kept the crow book a secret, even from Jacob and Malyssa. Until he knew more about what he was dealing with he didn't want to drag his friends into danger; they had already been through enough.

Winter came quickly and daylight came later and the night came earlier. His hours of studying the birds in the wild decreased dramatically.

Every few days, between lessons and football practice, he took himself to various parts of the woods, discretely watching crows.

It was a week before Christmas and most students were busily packing the bags to go home for the holidays, but not Billy. He had requested to stay with Jacob at school. Jacob had to stay now he had started at The Gifted Academy, otherwise there were too many mouths to feed, but he had so many family members at the academy, it was like a family Christmas holiday anyway.

Malyssa had to stay too, but she didn't want to. She was sick and unable to heal herself. Mr Leadbetter was treating her, but he needed to observe her throughout treatment. She was not the least bit happy with the thought of missing her mother's Christmas turkey with all the trimmings or opening one present on Christmas Eve whilst eating popcorn and watching a Christmas movie with her family.

Billy on the other hand, was looking forward to a festive Christmas and a real Christmas dinner. He actually felt sorry that his mother and sister wouldn't be having such a festive time.

Usually, their house was the house Christmas forgot. He and Jess would sing a few carols and make each other a gift or find something. Last year he gave Jess a pinecone he covered in glitter at school and explained to her that from the base she could see that it went in a Fibonacci spiral pattern. She didn't really care about his fact, but she loved the glitter. She watched it glisten in the light. She gave him a beautiful feather she found in the garden. Billy identified it as a Jay feather, with its contrasting black and white and striking blue patches.

This year he couldn't give her anything, and he just hoped without the added expense of him, their mother would get Jess at least something.

Billy was shaken from his memories by the familiar raucous of crows nearby. He stepped away from the small pond with a thick layer of ice and walked towards the sound. The crisp white snow crunched under his feet. Everywhere he looked was a hazy greyish brown, the odd speckle of green ivy in the tops of the trees and the bold red and green of holly splashed around tree stumps.

The snow had stopped falling and a thin layer of white covered the bare branches. In some places tall green conifers grew, looking strange without the usual lights and a star atop them like in the city back home. Animal tracks looped between trees.

He continued through the woodlands pulling his navy blue hat with a lighter rim tightly over his ears and wrapping himself more snuggly in his House coloured scarf, which matched his hat. It was double the thickness of the usual scarves and was beautifully knitted with the two blues together as one strand. The navy leather coat tied the blues in nicely and kept out the wind.

He quietly closed in on the family of crows making all the noise. He watched as they flapped their wings and huddled around another object. A closer inspection told Billy that the crows were crowded round a small Robin like a mob, pecking at it without mercy.

Billy raced at the flock and they took to the skies. But, Billy was too late; the small bird lay dead in the snow surrounded by its own orange-red mixed with brown and white feathers. Even the animal kingdom didn't seem to escape bullies.

Billy scooped the tiny bird up in his fingerless blue mix knitted gloves. He could feel the soft feathers on his fingers. It didn't seem fair to leave it out in the open, so he tucked it beneath a holly bush off the beaten track.

So far, Billy hadn't learned anything more about crows than Miss Leadbetter's book showed him, except that witnessing their attacks was worse than reading about them. Thank goodness his father had got to him sooner than he had got to the Robin! He made slow, sluggish tracks back to the main building.

The noise reduced dramatically come Christmas Eve. Most students and staff went home. The Leadbetters stayed. Miss Leadbetter lived on site anyway and Mr Leadbetter was treating Malyssa's ailments with one of his concoctions, although he would have likely stayed anyway with Brutus locked in the cabin in the woods. Billy doubted he'd take any chance leaving him alone - who else would administer the liquid suppressing his Manifestus?

Malyssa stopped sulking about having to stay now that she was feeling a little better. It probably helped that everyone slept in hammocks hanging from the beams in the Round Hall together. It was great mixing with the other Houses. Billy felt he was getting to know them better and he was having a wonderful family Christmas.

Sleeping in hammocks in the hall was only the tip of the iceberg for the wonders of Christmas at the academy. All the stops were pulled out at the most wonderful time of the year! The fairy lights from Harvest returned entwined around the beams once more, accompanied by sprigs of holly and the occasional mistletoe.

By the entrance a tall conifer was decorated with multi-coloured fairy lights; green, red and gold tinsel and silver baubles. Sitting at the top of the tree and shining brightly was a star. At the base of the tree, in beautiful coloured paper and ribbons covering the full spectrum of the rainbow, were presents of all sizes, likely for display purposes only, but it still looked magnificent. The tables were draped with pearlised red and green tablecloths.

Miss Leadbetter kept a few of the catering staff over the holidays and Billy could smell the delicious aromas they were creating in the kitchen. He couldn't remember a time Christmas had seemed to fill him with so much hope.

The large stone hearth on the opposite side of the hall to the entrance burned red hot and flames licked out at the stones and filled the hall with warmth and cast shadows over the walls that were much more easily seen now that the guardians had dwindled so much that their warriors were home for Christmas. It was only the guardians of those who stayed at the academy left.

Billy plonked himself at a table in Earth House area, where Jacob had purposely chosen to sit, saying, "It's nice to have a change of scenery, mix it up a bit!"

"Who's winning?" asked Billy, smiling as he perched on a chair to watch the card game.

"I am!" said Malyssa proudly and grinning at Jacob.

"Yeah, but only because I'm letting her...she's ill, I've got to cheer her up, haven't I?"

"What a load of rubbish, Jacob!" she reached over and

took one of the cards he held out facedown to her and added it to her own hand with a smile. Jacob frowned.

"I suppose you're letting her win too?" he asked the twins, Jacob's cousins, winking at them. They burst into laughter.

"We don't have to let her win!" said Simon.

"Yeah, Jacob's doing a good enough job letting her win by himself!" said James.

"He keeps getting left with the Joker!" added Simon. Billy joined in the laughter.

"Not all the time," said Jacob sulkily.

"But most of the time!" responded James.

"Well, he does make the best 'Old Maid' out of us, so if the hat fits..." Malyssa gestured to Jacob putting on a hat.

Simon thumped his hand on the table, his face creased with laughter lines, "Stop! Stop! You're killing me!"

"I take it you're feeling better, Malyssa?" asked Billy.

She nodded, "A lot better!"

It was nice to see her smiling again and Christmas wouldn't be good without her.

"Ooo, look out, Malyssa! Mr Leadbetter's on his way over here with that vial of pink liquid!" warned Simon.

"Oh, when will it be over?" she groaned loud enough

for Mr Leadbetter to hear.

"It will be over when you are completely well, without any snot or sniffles!"

Jacob cringed away from her, "And on that charming note I believe dinner is served."

They spent the rest of the evening eating drinking hot chocolate, playing games and generally being like they should be: excitable children on Christmas Eve!

Billy woke with a start early the next morning. Simon and James were already fighting over whose new scarf was whose despite the fact they were exactly the same! Billy rolled over to sit up, kicking something at the end of his bed. He rubbed his sleepy eyes.

"Merry Christmas, Billy" called Jacob pulling on a new pair of knitted House colour gloves.

"Merry Christmas, Jacob! Who are those from?"

"Mum made them. Look! She's even stitched leather patches to the fingertips and palms. These will be great for footy!" He pretended to dive for a ball, throwing himself on the floor and rolling.

"Nice save!" said Billy, laughing.

"Thanks. You not going to open your stocking, then?"

"My stocking?"

"Yeah, everyone who stays at the academy over Christmas gets one. It's from the academy."

Billy grabbed the red felt stocking. It had white trim and his name embroidered in gold across the white. Billy was thankful enough for the stocking, let alone its contents. He tipped it upside down whilst Jacob watched him.

"Great, isn't it?" said Jacob. "Chock-a-block full of chocolate! I love this place!"

It may have been only a quarter to six in the morning but Billy removed a red foil wrapper, and popped the chocolate in his mouth, "Mmmm...strawberry cream." His eyes twinkled with pleasure.

"You've got to check under the tree, too. I saw a couple of things for you."

Billy wasted no time, he swung himself out of the hammock, scattering chocolates and raced to the tree. Jacob's brother and sister were casually opening their gifts from their parents when Billy skidded over to them.

There they were: two presents with his name on, and one had a card attached. Both presents were wrapped in newspaper, but he didn't care, he couldn't wait to see what he'd been given. He tore the paper from the one without a card first. It was a jar full of angel shaped biscuits. There was a piece of brown string tied round the neck with a tag clearly made from a previous year's Christmas card.

Just as he was about to read it, Jacob called out with a mouthful of chocolate, "Who's it from?"

Billy read the tag aloud, "Dear Billy, thanks for looking after our little boy. Many blessings, Love Brenda Sole" followed by two kisses.

"Brenda Sole? That's Mum! Funny she sent you a present. Looking after me indeed! 'Little boy!' Pff! Hope you don't mind sharing Billy. Mum's biscuits are amazing!" He reached out to the jar and Billy jokingly slapped his hand away. Jacob pretended to cry.

Billy was already focussed on his next and last gift. He carefully peeled the sticky tape off that attached the envelope to the present, so that he didn't get a peak at the present until after he'd read what he assumed was a card rather than a letter, now that he held it.

He tore the envelope open. On the front of the card was a black silhouette of Jesus in a manger with Mary and Joseph either side of him; their heads tilted towards him. It was set against a blue starry background, with one larger gold star at the top of the card, presumably the North Star. Billy unfolded the card and began to read silently.

'Dear Billy,

Merry Christmas my lovely boy. I hope you're settling into The Gifted Academy well. The House isn't the same without you. Jess is certainly missing you. She wanted me to give you the white feather she found, so it's in the envelope.

I know I've not been much of a mum over the past few years, but your absence is making me reflect and change my ways. Being tired from work isn't an excuse for not spending time with my children.

You're my beautiful boy, with the biggest soul I've ever known. Remember that truth always, son. Remember who you are at all times.

Enjoy yourself! Family is those who choose to love you, and we love you lots, as I'm sure your friends there do. I'm trying to change, Billy, I promise.

Lots of love, hugs and kisses,

Mum and Jess x x x'

Jess had signed her own name in big crooked letters and added kisses just as big. Billy didn't know how to react to the letter. It was so different to what he was used to and it was still early days of this new side of his mum.

He closed the card and carefully placed it back in the envelope. He bent down to pick up the present. It was hard and fairly flat, like a book. He slowly pulled the paper off, not feeling the same excitement he was before the card.

At first he saw the back of a frame. The stand was flat against it. He turned it over and gasped. A hand flew to his mouth and a tear rolled down his cheek. It was a family photo. Billy was about six, his sister was a new-born baby and his mother was smiling so wide holding Jess...and his father stood behind him holding his shoulders tentatively. Billy sniffed.

"What did you get?" asked Jacob munching on one of Billy's biscuits.

"A photo of my family."

"Oh, that's nice."

"You have no idea," mumbled Billy staring into his father's dark brown eyes. His brown hair swept back behind his ears. Billy never realised how tall he was, Jess obviously took after him; but not Billy.

During the course of Christmas Day they ate a delicious turkey dinner, pulled crackers, sang carols and played games, and all the while there was a heaviness on Billy's heart distracting him from the merriment.

He went to bed with a full stomach and a full mind.

Billy kept his head down for the whole of the next term, putting all concerns other than his studies to the back of his mind and 'enjoying himself' just like his mother had told him too.

Chapter Sixteen

The Forest Cabin

It was the last weekend of the break between the spring and summer terms. Once again Billy, Malyssa, and the Sole family, plus a few others stayed at the academy.

"I can't believe I'm ill again," complained Malyssa throwing another snotty tissue into the wastebasket.

"I can!" said Jacob with a smile and a mischievous glint in his eye.

"And why is that?" said Malyssa, hands on her hips.

"Isn't it obvious?"

Malyssa looked at Billy, who shrugged his shoulders.

Jacob continued, "A nerd like you is allergic to holidays!" He fell about laughing, which was good or the tissue Malyssa threw would have caught him in the face rather than landing behind him.

"At least I can keep an eye on the two of you!" she said.

"On us?" questioned Jacob, fluttering his eyelids innocently. "We've been as good as gold for the last term. Billy hasn't been unconscious once!" He laughed again, but Billy didn't. Instead he was staring melancholy at the family photo he had propped up on his suitcase rather than leave in the dormitories over the holidays.

"You with us, Billy?" Jacob waved his arms in front of Billy's face, breaking him from reliving the fateful day his father died saving him.

"Oh, sorry. What did you say?"

"Malyssa was implying we get ourselves into trouble and she needs to keep an eye on us and I said we've had an eventful term, during which you've not been unconscious once!" He couldn't help but find himself hilarious the second time around too.

"Ha-ha!" said Billy sarcastically. Billy quickly changed his disposition into one of concern.

"What? Why has your face changed?" asked Jacob.

"It has been uneventful, hasn't it?"

"Yes, but that's a good thing," said Malyssa.

266

"Yes, I know, but we haven't gone to the cabin once to check on..." he whispered the name, "...Brutus."

"Why would we need to?" asked Jacob, drumming his fingers on the table they were sat round before bed.

"I don't know, I just think we should check on him. See if we can learn anything new."

Malyssa was about to object, but was interrupted by Mr Leadbetter entering the hall and calling, "Lights out! Come on! Into bed everyone!" He immediately flicked out the main lights and the students had to stumble through the dark to their sleeping bags lying on the hammocks - good job they'd had a lot of practice.

It didn't take long for Billy to fall, exhausted into a deep slumber.

In his dream there was an eerie darkness covering the land. Moonlight caught the edges of spider like branches that scratched his face as he raced through them. He kept peering over his shoulder. Footsteps thudded behind him, and the faint outline of a figure following through the woodlands.

Billy was panting heavily; he had been running for some time. He had no idea where he was running to or who he was running from.

THWACK! He tripped over a tree root or log or rock

and landed face down in snow. He scrambled to his feet, brushing his icy hands on the back of his trousers, but it didn't really help.

He saw a warm yellow glow in the distance. Now he had an aim, a direction to run in. Snow started to lightly dust him and his surroundings. His teeth chattered together as he carried himself swiftly between black trees.

The cabin. It was the cabin that was the warm glow. He could see the silhouette of it. It was unmistakable with its bowed slanting roof. The light was coming from the window he had peered through in the past.

He came to the barbed-wire fence. His fingers were nearly numb with cold. He fiddled with the fence trying to make a gap, but he misjudged it and it caught his face as he ducked through. He felt it rip through his flesh despite how cold his face was.

He contemplated trying to hide in the bushes, but he would easily be found. They were gaining on him fast.

They made no noise except for their footfalls and their heavy breathing.

Billy would have to go into the cabin. He would explain what he was doing their later, but at least he would be safe with Mr Leadbetter; he was a strong warrior.

He advanced on the cabin. He used the rotting banister to pull himself to his feet. He reached for the door handle, but there was a padlock. He whimpered fearful of being caught with nowhere to go. He shook the padlock urgently and realised it wasn't closed. Mr Leadbetter must just use it as a deterrent. He pulled it off and threw it into the nearby bushes, not wanting to be locked inside the cabin.

He whipped open the cabin door and slammed it closed, his back leaning against it. He kept his eyes closed, whilst he panted against the door.

The cabin was oddly quiet, just the crackle of firewood, his beating heart and deep breathing. He slowly opened his eyes. There was a wooden chair in the centre of the room. Pieces of rope dangled from the arms and legs and tangled around the seat. The seat was...empty!

Brutus should have been sitting tied to the wooden chair, but he wasn't there. That's when Billy noticed the smashed table. The rough plywood shelves were hanging from the walls; one was broken in two on the floor. Tin cups and a dented kettle were sprawled on the wooden floorboards, and a bucket of water lie spilt by the sink.

A tinge of blue suddenly caught Billy's eye from behind the busted workbench. He tiptoed over to peer behind the bench. He yelped in horror and went to make a dash for the door again. But it was too late. Brutus burst through the cabin door shrieking with laughter. The door clanged loudly and came off its top hinge. Chunks of wet, rotten wood dropped to the floor.

"I see you've found my brother!" An evil smirk spread across his demented face. Billy had not noticed the scarring on the right side of his face before. "Oh, Master will be pleased I caught you! And I got rid of him too!" He pointed a foot in Mr Leadbetter's direction.

Sparks went off in Billy's brain, 'Master'. He'd heard that name before, but where? No matter how much he searched his mind the answer wouldn't come.

Billy backed up into the corner of the cabin. Brutus advanced with his hands outstretched. Billy screamed. Everything went black.

Billy awoke the next morning panting and dripping in a cold sweat. "No! No! He's escaped! He's escaped!" His screams filled the Round Hall.

"Billy! Billy! Settle down, Mate!" Jacob rushed to his side and patted Billy on the back gently.

"Who's escaped?" yelled Priscilla through a stifled yawn.

"Probably his stupid frog!" croaked Peter annoyed at

being woken up in such a dramatic way.

Mr Leadbetter came flying into the hall, "What's wrong? I heard screaming!" His usually immaculate blue mohican was squashed in different directions and he was wrapped in a navy blue robe over his striped pyjamas.

Once over his initial shock at seeing Mr Leadbetter in nightwear, Jacob answered, "Um...nothing is wrong, Sir," he rubbed his head searching his own tired thoughts, "Billy just had a bad dream, that's all...woke us all up screaming."

"Is that true Billy?" He scrutinised Billy's face, which was pale in the morning light and beads of sweat clung to his skin.

"Yes, Sir." Billy barely breathed the words, but was understood by his nodding head.

"OK, well if you insist everything is fine..." he didn't finish his sentence, just yawned, turned and walked away.

By this point everyone sleeping in the Round Hall was wide awake and began playing around, much to Peter's horror who would have liked to have spent the morning lazing in bed peacefully. The noise provided the much-needed cover for Malyssa and Jacob to interrogate Billy.

"Mate, you OK?" He stood towering over Billy, "You gave us a fright; and I was playing an exceptionally good game of football in my dream." He stared into the inner thoughts of his mind, smiling.

"Of course, he's not alright, Jacob! How many dreams do you wake from screaming and then feel 'OK'?" Malyssa stood on the opposite side of Billy's hammock to Jacob rubbing Billy's back calmly with one hand. She looked at him concerned. "How *are* you feeling, Billy?"

"We need to check the cabin today!" he said throwing himself out of bed.

"What are you talking about? We can't go to the cabin. We should be having fun - it's the holidays! We've been good, we deserve to have fun!" said Jacob.

"Let him explain, Jacob! Go ahead, Billy - why do we have to go to the cabin?"

Billy was quickly changing into a shirt and trousers whilst they talked to him. He answered whilst sitting on the floor trying to jam his left foot into his right boot.

"Wrong foot," said Jacob.

"Thanks," replied Billy.

"Billy, will you please explain!" Malyssa felt less empathy now and more impatience.

"You'd better tell her, Mate, Malyssa's pulling the same face my mum does just before she clouts us with the oven mitt!" He feigned fear of Malyssa, who glared at him and crossed her arms.

"You're only adding to the similarity," said Jacob followed by a wink.

She turned her attention back to Billy, "Stop putting your boots on and talk to us, if we're coming - you need to tell us where."

"The cabin, I told you!"

"OK, so you did, but why?"

"He's escaped!"

"Who has?"

"Brutus!"

Malyssa and Jacob exchanged glances, and Jacob spoke up first, "How do you know?"

"I dreamt it!"

"It was a dream, Billy. You said it yourself," said Jacob.

"It felt real! I need to check!"

"You can't go now, what will you say to Mr Leadbetter? He doesn't know we know about Brutus."

Billy thought for a moment, "I'll tell him we're going for a walk."

"It's nearly breakfast; no-one is going to believe that Jacob went for a walk instead of having breakfast," Malyssa said, smirking in Jacob's direction.

"Hey!" said Jacob defensively.

"'Hey' what? It's true," responded Malyssa.

"Just 'hey'." Jacob was defeated.

Billy paid little attention to their squabbles. "But, we must check. It doesn't feel right...I need to know if it was just a dream for sure." He tied his bootlaces with less urgency knowing he wouldn't be going anytime soon because of breakfast.

"Agreed, we need to make sure, but we can't draw attention to ourselves." She pushed her glasses up the bridge of her nose.

"What about between breakfast and lunch?" suggested Jacob.

"Maybe, but these guys wanted to finish the five thousand piece puzzle of the Ocean Giants, and you both said you would help this morning. It could take all day," Malyssa reminded them. "We could go tonight, under cover of darkness." Malyssa held a hand to her mouth and started coughing.

"You, OK? Need some water?" asked Billy concerned. He looked at Jacob and knew by his expression that they were thinking the same thing: Malyssa was not well enough to come, but how would they tell her?

"When will we set off?" she asked, followed by more

coughs and splutters.

"Um...midnight," lied Billy.

He and Jacob spent the rest of the day being cagey with Malyssa under the false pretence of not being overheard. Part of him felt guilty for lying to his friend, but the other part, the bigger part, felt protective.

After the previous night's dream and what he expected to find or *not* find at the cabin, Billy was in no mood to sleep that night, even if it was only for a few hours before they snuck out. He checked his watch sporadically tilting it towards the lamplight he shone into his sleeping bag.

The watch was incredibly worn, the face was scratched beyond repair and the strap was worn and cracked.

At eleven o'clock precisely he slid out of the hammock and tiptoed over to Jacob, who was snoring loudly. He felt mean for waking him but more important things were at stake. He shook Jacob. Jacob gasped and began to say, "What? What?" too loudly for Billy's liking.

Billy clamped a hand over Jacob's mouth. "Shhh! It's eleven o'clock, we need to go."

Jacob had slept fully clothed like Billy. He sluggishly rolled off of his hammock and the pair crept by moonlight out of the Round Hall and out of the building.

The weather may have been starting to warm u at this time of year, but at one hour until midnight, it was still chilly enough to cause goose bumps.

"Come on, we'll go through the 5-a-side pitch like before," directed Billy to a very groggy Jacob.

The wind worked its way into their bones as they ran over the open space. They were pleased to seek shelter from the cruel wind in the dark woodlands despite its long uninviting branches. It was the only woodland on the academy grounds that looked like it was dying even in the season of life and growth, as if the very ground it grew on and where Billy walked was cursed to never know the beauty of life.

"Billy" called Jacob over the creepy noises of the forest.

"What?" he replied in a loud whisper hoping Jacob would follow suit.

"Have you ever wondered why this woodland is never lit up with fairy lights and lamp stands like the others?"

"Probably because they don't want students to find the cabin."

"Yes, but, no students, except for us, ever enter these woods and there's no official rule not to, people just...don't." Jacob jumped and a little squeal escaped him as a little twig fell landing on his head and dropped onto his face.

"Shh!" Billy was unsympathetic, focussed solely on the task ahead.

"Sorry," muttered Jacob.

The woods seemed different to the last time Billy had been there and certainly unfamiliar to his dream. Maybe the others were right and this was a fool's errand and they would reach the cabin and Brutus was asleep tied to the chair just as before.

Billy suddenly wondered if Mr Leadbetter ever let him loose to wander or had extended the ropes that bound him or chained him on a long chain. He wasn't used to the treatment of prisoners, but still, Brutus was Mr Leadbetter's brother.

Suddenly, images from his dream filled his mind; Mr Leadbetter lying lifeless on the wooden flooring of the cabin and Brutus advancing, towering over him.

"Come on! We need to hurry!" Billy got a new spurt on.

"I'm going as fast as I can! I'm taller than you and all those branches you duck under, well, let's just say, they seem to like my face."

Billy had noticed that Jacob used even more humour

when he was scared, and felt a sudden twinge in his chest.

"Jacob, thanks for coming with me."

"Sure, sure, what are Mates for, if not for joining you on a mission to locate a crazy evil man in the middle of a creepy wood, in the middle of the night?" He waved his arms around removing spider webs.

As they drew closer to the cabin the ground soon turned to mud. It sucked at Billy's heels as he slogged across the swampy ground.

Rain began to patter to the dirt floor. There was the crack of a branch breaking in the distance. Billy squeezed himself between the barbed wire quickly as the patter of rain turned to larger splatters.

In the time it took Billy and Jacob to reach the shelter of the cabin porch, the rain had turned heavy and lightning lit up the sky. Jacob squealed as a mouse shot across his foot, the stoop and into a crack in the cabin wall.

Billy peered in through a dirty window on the porch; inside was dimly lit by the fire. Dead flies and a curled up wasp were on the windowsill, but there, in the centre of the room, was Brutus, his chin resting on his chest. Billy stared at the side of his head and exhaled deeply in relief.

Suddenly, Brutus turned and stared directly at him.

Billy nearly jumped out of his skin and his scream was loud enough to wake the dead.

Brutus furrowed his brow, before scowling. His greasy black hair dangled in his face.

"We'd better go!" urged Jacob tugging on Billy's arm.

Billy shook him off. "No!"

"But, he's seen us, and definitely heard us! We need to get out of here!"

"I'm going in," said Billy shuffling towards the door. He stared at the large padlock.

"You can't go in there! Firstly, it's crazy, and secondly, the door is padlocked."

"But, I don't think…" Billy reached for the padlock and fiddled with it, "…it is." The padlock was loose, merely a deterrent like in his dream. He pulled it off and dropped it to the ground.

"If you're seriously going in, I'm waiting out here, where it's safer." A screech sounded, like that of a pursued animal. Jacob shuddered. "I'd still take a hungry wolf over him!" He pointed at Brutus.

"OK, you keep an eye out for Mr Leadbetter. I'm going in." Billy pulled on the door. It stuck a little before creaking open. The warmth from the fire hit him but not as much as the foul stench of body odour. Billy gingerly crossed the cabin floor leaving muddy boot prints, until he faced Brutus at a safe distance away.

"Well, well! Look who it is! William Wortol! And I thought I'd have to find you, and here we are, with you having found me." He gave Billy a curled, yellow-toothed grin.

Billy noticed that half of Brutus' face was badly scarred; probably from the fire he had survived.

"How do you know who I am?" Billy asked more boldly than he felt.

"I follow The Beast, and we all know you!" He licked his lips.

"You remember the crows and creatures when you were little...the ones that killed 'Daddy Dearest'?" Billy balled his hands into fists. He wasn't usually one for violence, but something about Brutus, even before mentioning his father, made his blood boil.

"Hit a nerve, did I?" Brutus laughed and continued, "I was there. Not with the crows, no, I was hiding in the trees past the lake. You remember the lake, don't you, Billy?"

Billy's fingernails dug into his palms.

"Clearly, you do, but just in case you don't: it's the lake where 'Daddy' died saving you!" He spat on the floor, disgusted. "You have that feather on your arm, a symbol of power and greatness, and you choose to suppress it and be a frog! A frog of all things!" He was beginning to shout. "Could be worse, you could be a bug!" He looked deep into Billy's eyes, "I don't know why Master let you live that day, or this long! I'd have let you drown!"

"It wasn't his choice!" cried Billy, "My father saved me!"

"Master called us off! Told us not to touch you! He wanted you alive!"

"Then why did he try to kill me?"

"He wasn't trying to kill *you*! You were just the bait!"

The news crashed over Billy like waves. He staggered back to the workbench.

"When The Beast wants something done, he does *not* fail! As I said, I don't know why he let you live! The Beast should have drowned you! I'd have gladly done it for him!"

An angry tear rolled down Billy's cheek.

"You should be dead like that Humanum that mother of yours married! She's a disgrace! Marries a Humanum and then lives like one!"

That was the last straw for Billy. He hurled himself at Brutus knocking the chair backwards to the floor. The sound of wood splintering and crashing filled the cabin. Billy pummelled Brutus with his tiny fists barely making an impact, whilst Brutus howled with menacing laughter.

Billy was so full of rage punching Brutus he didn't realise that the rope shackles that bound Brutus no longer restrained him, but, fortunately, someone had.

Jacob had been keeping a watchful eye on the surroundings of the cabin, especially after the animal cries he had heard, but the crash of Brutus and Billy to the ground grabbed his attention. He looked through the murky window, yelling Billy's name.

Without a second thought, he burst into the cabin. He tried to haul Billy off of Brutus before Brutus was able to capture Billy. "Billy! Get off him! We need to go! Now!"

Billy punched and kicked wildly. Jacob grabbed him round the middle and pulled him back until Billy only had a grip on Brutus' collar. He eventually lost his grip.

The Beast is coming for us, Billy! He will get his way!" Brutus started to scramble slowly and weakly to his feet.

Before Jacob could stop him, Billy grabbed the old oil lamp and lobbed it into the fireplace. Jacob grabbed him and pushed him towards the sink, "Manifest, now!" he yelled at Billy.

They fully manifested just in time for Jacob to pull

them in the direction of the plughole. Even if Brutus could manifest, he would be too big to follow them. They hurtled through the drainpipes, being twisted and turned every which way, before landing with a splash in the wastewater pool on the mud outside the cabin. They quickly manifested back into human form. "Run!" screamed Jacob, "The cabin will blow!"

The rain had stopped but the wind was still howling through the trees. Just as they reached the far side of the football pitch an explosion painted the night sky orange.

Ears ringing, Jacob pulled Billy in a different direction back to the main building shouting, "They'll all be coming that way - it's the quickest! They can't see us like this! We will go through these woods! They're well lit so keep out of sight as best you can!"

Billy followed Jacob, not really getting a word Jacob said.

At the other end of the woods they saw the coast was clear. Billy peeked round the corner to the main walk way to see the backs of students and the two Leadbetters.

Billy turned to climb the steps to sneak back into the building while it was vacant. It wasn't as vacant as he thought it was. At the top of the steps in white and silver striped pyjamas and square spectacles, stood an unimpressed Malyssa.

"You went without me," she said calmly. Billy couldn't hear her too well, but he could see she wasn't shouting at him.

"Sorry!" he shouted back in his near deafness.

Malyssa stared at him and then at Jacob with cold, hard and flinty eyes before slamming the door behind her as she stomped back into the building through to the Round Hall.

Billy and Jacob's clothes were wet. They went to the toilet and shower facilities where they had left their pyjamas to change into. They had already kicked their muddy boots off at the main entrance so they didn't leave a trail.

Billy's hearing was gradually coming back but it was still accompanied by ringing.

"We need to go speak to Malyssa," said Jacob.

"Let me apologise first. It was my idea to go without her," said Billy leading the way back to the hall.

Malyssa sat at a table just inside the doors waiting for them; her shoulders drooped.

Billy spoke first, "I'm sorry we lied to you, Malyssa."

She rose her head, her bottom lip trembling, "Why did you lie to me?"

"We didn't think you were well enough to come with us - "

"Yeah, and I'm glad you didn't! We nearly died!" added Jacob.

"So I heard."

"I don't mean the explosion, I mean Brutus! He's not tied up anymore!"

Malyssa looked concerned, "So, your dream was right? He's escaped?" she said to Billy.

"Not exactly," said Jacob, shuffling his feet awkwardly.

"What do you mean?" Malyssa's brow furrowed.

"He means: he hadn't escaped until I helped him escape by smashing the chair when I attacked him." Billy avoided her gaze.

Malyssa sighed. "Are you hurt?" she asked.

"Yes. I hurt all over," said Billy. Jacob nodded.

"Come, let me heal you." She gestured with her hands for them to come forward.

"You're not mad?"

"Oh, I'm still hurt, but my Manifestum nature is to heal. It's my true self and it's as though I am compelled to act on it."

Chapter Seventeen
Man Hunt

"Have you two heard anything about Brutus?" said Billy leaning forward and sliding his chair closer to Jacob and Malyssa in weapons study class. They were supposed to be copying a picture from their textbooks and making notes on uses, appearance, how to use and so forth.

"No," said Malyssa.

Jacob shook his head.

"I assume you still aren't suspected for the explosion?" asked Malyssa.

"No. The rumour for the last two weeks is it was caused by methane bubbling from the bottom of the lake and lightning striking the lake in a freak act of nature."

Billy continued to sketch the steel blade of an axe. He spoke in a low voice to make sure it went under the radar of the rest of the class, who were all chatting anyway. Apparently, Mr Nelson preferred a bubbly class to the silence some of the other teachers preferred, as long as they were working of course.

"Mr Leadbetter obviously wants the fact that there was a cabin kept under wraps," stated Jacob, briefly ceasing to draw, unable to multitask. "The methane explosion seems to be the reason that students aren't allowed to go wandering off alone," said Malyssa, "although I can't believe people are buying that reason, I mean even with a teacher with us, if an explosion happens, we'd still be blown to smithereens, wouldn't we!"

Jacob shook his head in disbelief, "Charming Malyssa."

"Well, it's true," she offered more quietly.

Billy raised his eyes from his book to Mr Nelson, who was making the rounds throughout the class to each semi-circular wooden desk. The grand glass construction, a bit like a giant greenhouse, that Weapons Study took place in absorbed the sun's rays and warmth. The room was always hot. In winter heat radiated from the lamps, which hung from the beams. Mr Nelson never seemed to handle the heat particularly well and spent a majority of the lesson fanning himself with a book. Most of the time he looked like a flower dressed in green with his ginger hair and red face.

Billy watched him tug at his collar and suddenly a spark went off in his mind about the night Brutus escaped.

"The tattoo!" he exclaimed, a little too loud for Jacob and Malyssa's liking, who both put a finger to their lips and shushed him.

"I saw Brutus' tattoo, well...sort of...like Mr and Miss Leadbetters'...except it looked the same...but different somehow." He scratched his head as he searched the inner pictures of his mind.

"Maybe, if they all have it, it's a family thing," suggested Malyssa.

"But, if it's a 'family thing'," Jacob made air quotation marks with his fingers around 'family things', then why is Brutus' slightly different?" questioned Jacob.

"Well, I never really got a good look at any of them, to be honest," said Billy, beginning to look a little flushed himself, "but Mr and Miss Leadbetter both covered theirs as soon as they saw me looking."

"I agree, it's intriguing," said Malyssa.

"*Intriguing indeed*," mocked Jacob. "Talk like a normal kid."

"Like you, you mean?" responded Malyssa shirty, "Fine! Yeah Mate, you're right!" She mimicked Jacob's voice.

"I don't sound like that – "

"Guys! You're getting away from the point," interrupted Billy before a blood bath broke out. "The point is they must mean something and I sort of remember seeing them, so maybe you could tell me what they mean?"

"Fine." Jacob and Malyssa poked their tongues out at each other.

"It looked like some kind of lettering with black wings coming from it...maybe a an 'H' or an 'A' or an 'M'."

"It was an 'M'," said Malyssa, a tremble in her voice.

"How do you know?' Billy cocked his head to one side.

Malyssa took a deep breath, held it a couple of seconds and exhaled before she began to explain, "When the academy was first started, the 'M', standing for 'Manifestum', with white wings was the academy emblem, but," she breathed heavily again, "When The Beast came to power, his was changed to black wings like his crow Manifestus and became the symbol for his followers to know one another." She shuddered.

"So, the academy changed their emblem?" asked Jacob, unaware of the history.

"Yes. More importantly, you said you saw it on Headmistress Leadbetter and Mr Leadbetter. Are you sure?"

"I definitely saw something like that."

Malyssa twirled her hair and nudged her spectacles higher on her nose and they fell silent contemplating.

Billy eventually broke the silence, "I say we go find Brutus!"

"What?"

"Why?"

"They obviously haven't caught him yet because we have to be accompanied by a teacher everywhere. And as far as we know it's only the Leadbetters who know he's here, so it's only them looking for him and..." he trailed off and stared at the floor.

"And?" probed Malyssa.

"And...it's my fault he's loose." He ran a hand through his blonde curls.

"You're going to no matter what we say, aren't you?"

said Malyssa knowingly.

Billy nodded.

"Then I guess, you can count me in, Mate," said Jacob less than enthusiastically.

"Me too," sighed Malyssa.

"If you don't want to come, don't come. I won't force you."

"I've got to stop you from getting killed," stated Jacob, a small smile on his face.

"And you keep needing healing, for some reason." Malyssa smirked at Jacob. "What would he do without us?"

"He wouldn't have made it past the first day!" said Jacob beginning to laugh.

"OK, OK, you're right," Billy conceded. "We'll go tonight, after dinner."

"What about the others in the dorms? They'll see we're missing." Malyssa was swinging her feet under the table and they tapped against her stool.

"Stuff your sleeping bag so it looks like you're in it," suggested Jacob quicker than expected. He held his hands out to his sides gesturing for them to look at him, "Hey! I live in a House full of people at home; sometimes I need some quiet time!"

All three started laughing drawing attention to themselves.

"What exactly is so funny about the axe?" Mr Nelson stared at them each in turn. He mopped his brow with a hanky, making him a lot less intimidating, although his leaf style green suede blazer and trousers already gave him a less than terrifying appearance. It was hard to believe that he was one of the best warriors in the country to be working at The Gifted Academy.

"Nothing, Sir," all three responded simultaneously.

Mr Nelson's nose twitched and his moustache wriggled like a furry caterpillar. Jacob had to look away to stifle a laugh. They needed to laugh whilst they could, that night could change everything.

They reconvened after dinner outside the academy building with the rest of the academy to be escorted to their dormitories.

"Where do you think he'll be?" asked Jacob, a faint warble to his voice.

"I think he's still in the cabin woodlands. There's no lights over there remember," replied Billy. He shivered in his cardigan. He forgot how chilly it was once the sun went down, even more so in the Manifestum realm. They slipped away quietly from their Houses. Malyssa's dormitory was in the opposite direction to Billy and Jacob's, so she decided to back track as soon as Mr Fusion, Mr Grasp and Miss Shuttle started leading Air House away.

The three of them walked briskly through the well-lit woodlands trying their best to keep out of sight. They crossed the 5-a-side football pitch, which was dry underfoot for a change. At least things were going well so far.

They still had to make it across the field to the woods before they could be covered by the shadow of darkness.

"It's a big wood, where should we start?" asked Malyssa, already feeling a little breathless being as she didn't enjoy being as active as Billy and Jacob.

A flash of white light suddenly rose up from the region where the cabin had been. "There!" responded both Billy and Jacob in unison.

They stepped through the barrier of darkness into the woods. A sudden drop in the temperature made the hairs on the back of Billy's neck stand on end.

"I don't like this," whispered Malyssa, "it doesn't feel right." She stood close to Billy and he could feel her trembling.

"You can go back if you want, Malyssa," suggested Billy. He was well aware of the eerie feeling she talked of.

"Or...wait here for us to come back," offered Jacob. He wanted her to be safe, but he also liked the idea that she was nearby if, or more likely *when*, he needed healing. It was selfish, he knew, but he couldn't help it, fear had gripped him and his survival instincts had kicked in.

"No, I'm coming with you. I just don't like it is all, she replied. She took a deep breath trying to calm herself. It didn't appear to be working.

Together they delved deeper into the woods. They followed the same beaten track as in the past, but it seemed different to them...unknown. They ducked under branches that seemed to come out of nowhere, and tripped over logs in their path. They came across an opening in the trees.

"Stay quiet," said Billy, stepping out first. His foot snapped a twig sounding as loud as a gunshot in the stillness and silence.

"This isn't right," he said, "we must have gone off the track." He stared to the other side of the opening he had just stepped into.

A figure stepped out from between the trees. Moonlight struck him picking up the chiselled nose, the unshaven face and bristly black hair that curtained his savage face. Black leather draped the figure. He snarled, his mouth a muzzle of yellow fangs. He lifted his face to the moon. He let out a monstrous howl, before fixing his eyes back on his prey and licking his lips.

"That's not Brutus," muttered Jacob, pointing out the obvious.

The hideous figure suddenly manifested. The fur sprouted on him, thick and black. A wolf glowered before them like none Billy had seen in books. It slowly advanced on them, growling. The closer it got, the more saliva dripped from its jaw. Billy, Jacob and Malyssa were frozen with fear.

Another white flash suddenly rose up further into the woods, breaking the trance like state.

Billy's mind worked on over drive on a plan. They couldn't manifest because Jacob would literally be a fish out of water, whether he semi or fully manifested. Billy recalled all the facts he could about wolves that he'd read in a matter of seconds. Their lives depended on it.

He whispered quickly to Jacob and Malyssa. He knew the wolf would have excellent hearing, but maybe the speed at which he spoke would distort his words.

"They run on instincts!" he said as fast as he could

hoping the others could keep up with his speech. "Hopefully, his animal part is stronger than his human part right now and we can use that against him."

"How?" asked Malyssa.

Great, they heard and understood me! "Wolves usually work in a pack, but he's on his own."

"So?" said Jacob, his knees beginning to knock together as he stared at the wolf's yellow eyes.

"He *should* instinctively go for the weakest prey. If we split up he will chase only one of us: the weakest."

They all knew Malyssa was the weakest. She was the smallest, least athletic and slower than Billy and Jacob.

She gulped. "Fine...get ready to run." She began to countdown, "Three, two, one, run!" she yelled. She purposely and bravely ran a little towards the wolf to definitely get his attention.

After a split second of confusion, the wolf chose his instincts and leapt after Malyssa, leaving Billy and Jacob sprinting along different routes towards where they had seen the second flash of light.

They kept running for a long time. Billy's chest was getting sore in the cold air. He heard footsteps padding through the woods behind him. He turned to look, but couldn't see anything - SMACK!

"Ow!"

Billy recognised the voice instantly belonging to Jacob, even before he'd seen whom he had collided with. "Quick! Climb the tree! Someone's coming from that way!" Billy pointed in the direction from which he came.

"I-heard-two-voices-coming-from-behind-me," said Jacob between pants for breath.

"Jacob, boost me up! Quick!"

Billy then scrambled his way to the highest point of the tree. He wanted to Manifest, but it wouldn't be fair to leave Jacob like a lamb to the slaughter. He had to be brave for his friend, especially as Jacob had valiantly followed him into danger.

They watched from the top of the tree. The wolf had been hot on Billy's heels, having lost Malyssa, but lost their trail near the tree too. The wolf transformed into the grizzly man. Billy wasn't sure which was scarier: man or beast.

"Where is he, Flint?" bellowed a voice strangely recognisable to Billy.

"I followed his scent to this tree, Master" growled Flint, the wolf Manifestus.

"Get him!" shrieked the newcomer.

Billy shuddered with panic. He recognised the black

feathers.

"I can't climb that high, Master; it won't hold my weight." He dropped his head in shame.

"You stupid - "

"Wait!" snapped the third man, "I see the other boy!"

Billy recognised the snivelling voice; it belonged to Brutus.

"I can get him!"

Billy and Jacob had nowhere to move to that was any safer than where they were. They had to stay still and await their fate.

Billy saw the glint of metal in Brutus' hand too late. The dagger flew through the branches, piercing Jacob's thigh and knocking him backwards off the branch, howling with pain.

"Jacob!" screamed Billy. Without a second thought he dived headfirst out of the tree after him. He managed to grab Jacob's feet and expected to plummet face first into the woodland floor.

But, neither he nor Jacob hit the ground. They hovered in mid-air. Billy looked over his shoulder to see two large shimmering white wings. They were twice the size of him, protruding from his back. Jacob still screamed in agony and fear as he dangled above the three evil men below.

Billy smiled at them and disappeared in a cloud of feathers over the treetops before he dropped quickly below the surface to keep out of sight. He placed Jacob by the entrance to the woods. "Hang in there, Jacob," he said propping him up against a tree, "I'm sure Malyssa will find you." But he wasn't even sure Malyssa was alive.

Billy flew back to the men, directed by their angry voices. He landed a little bit away and approached on foot. He saw Brutus and The Beast standing over the body of Flint. He could see the arrow sticking out of Flint's chest and the bow still in The Beast's claw like grip.

Billy coughed. The two men suddenly looked up. The Beast grinned from ear to ear. He was in the hideous Semi-Manifested form Billy had seen before in his bedroom during the attack. The long crooked beak-like nose; large black feathered wings above clawed feet. He resembled an immortal beast from ancient myths.

Billy was flooded with fear. His heart raced, nearly exploding. He tapped his thumb alternately with his index and middle fingers trying to soothe himself. It was not an easy feat standing in front of two scary evil men, especially when he realised he had forgotten a weapon.

Chapter Eighteen

The Beast

The Beast pulled a black arrow from his quiver and readied his bow. He drew back the string and aimed it at Billy, but he held the bow steady without releasing the arrow.

Billy stood his ground despite the empty feeling in the pit of his stomach and the desire to flee. He knew he had to stop The Beast and Brutus.

The Beast laughed arrogantly. "You're a boy, all alone now, with no weapon, against two armed men and yet you stand before us as bold as brass. I must applaud your bravery," he implored.

"I don't want your applause!" Billy stared back into

The Beast's beady eyes as he glared at him down his beaky nose, a smug grin forming below it.

"How dare you speak - " spat Brutus stepping forward.

"Wait!" ordered The Beast, "Leave him!"

"But, Master, he needs to know his place."

"And so do you, my friend!" he screamed at Brutus.

"Yes, Master," said Brutus bowing his head, "Sorry."

Brutus' buckling posture before The Beast struck a cord in Billy, like he'd felt the same, but he couldn't place the memory. It could have been a trick of his brain.

Billy found it hard to believe that Brutus was the same man he'd fought in the cabin, the way he snivelled around The Beast.

"So, Billy, we finally meet again." The Beast's tone was almost friendly.

"You know who I am?" Billy raised an eyebrow.

"I told you he was coming for you!" sneered Brutus.

"Shut up! I wasn't talking to the monkey, when the organ grinder is right here!" commanded Billy, trying to get a rise out of Brutus.

"Why you little – " Brutus was steaming, but he held himself back under orders. "Kill him, Master! Do it now!"

"Fine. If I must," he responded flippantly.

Billy dropped to the ground and rolled. He heard the bow string twang, and the arrow whistle and thud. He opened his tightly squeezed-shut eyes.

Brutus was staggering around, his mouth open and his eyes glazed. He fell backwards hitting a tree and collapsed at its base, the black arrow sticking out of his chest. It was in the dead centre of his heart.

Billy stared, eyes wide. "W-why did you do that?" he stammered. His mouth felt dry.

"Would you rather I'd have shot you? I have more arrows...if you wish - " He reached for another.

"No!" interrupted Billy.

"Very well." The Beast let his arms fall to his side.

"I-I don't understand," said Billy shaking his head. He raised himself slowly back to his feet.

Standing opposite The Beast, he couldn't understand how he had gained so much power and so many followers; he wasn't particularly tall or well-built, although he was terrifyingly menacing.

"He's done his job and not very well. I no longer need him now that I have you."

"But, why do you want me? I'm no-one. I'm just a boy." Billy could feel his limbs trembling with both cold and fear.

"Just a boy?" The Beast laughed at the sheer utterance of such a ludicrous notion. "You're not *just* a boy!" He smiled at Billy, his face softer than before. "You're *my* boy!"

Billy's thoughts began to spin. "Y-you tried to kill me...several times. You c-can't be my father!"

"Oh, but I am, Son," he declared. "And did I try to kill you? Are you sure?" He cocked his head.

"Yes!" shouted Billy, "First, when I was little! Then you attacked me in my bedroom! And it must have been you who put Chelsea Grease up to warping the weather, trying to kill me in a storm!"

The Beast scoffed. "You think some silly little girl was creating that storm. It takes an experienced Weather Warper to do that. I had Flint do it...he *was* one of the best."

"So, you *were* trying to kill me - like I said!"

Billy's tremble started to subside and a warming anger began to course through his body.

The Beast smiled as he watched Billy's anger build. "The storm was for those Leadbetters! They thought they could help their dear brother, Brutus, and I was showing they would never win! I always have the upper hand!" he growled.

"The attack on me and my sister was definitely intended!"

"Yes! On *that* girl!"

"My sister, Jess," stressed Billy.

The Beast nearly choked when Billy claimed Jess as his sister. "She's in the way of your destiny! She's distracting you! And she's not your sister! You are of my blood!" He spat on the ground with disgust, like just mentioning her left a nasty taste in his mouth.

"What about when you nearly drowned me, when I was little?" Billy yelled at him accusingly.

"I saved you!" bellowed The Beast.

"Saved me? Saved me! You chased me onto the ice, and not just you!"

"We've been through this before!"

"No we haven't!"

"Yes, last year, my dear boy. You were with me. The people you *trust* to look after you have clearly hidden your memories, poking around your mind and you're yelling at me!"

"You're a liar!"

"I lifted you to the surface of the water! I placed you in that foolish Humanum's hand before holding him under the water! Always a bonus to have two Manifestus' isn't it?" he winked at Billy.

"You killed my father!" Billy shook violently with rage.

"I am your father!"

"My father's dead!"

"That Humanum was *not* your father and he was meant to die!"

Billy didn't know how to respond, his chest moved up and down as he breathed deeply. He clenched his jaw until it hurt.

"Come with me," The Beast held out a pale withered hand.

Billy stepped and stumbled backwards, his legs answering for him.

The Beast stepped towards him, closing the gap. "We will be great together! Powerful! Unstoppable, when I train you. Come, rule by my side, Son. Inherit everything! All the kingdoms!" He offered his hand again.

"NEVER!" Billy hollered.

The Beast's mouth distorted into an ugly twist. "If you're not with me; you're against me!"

Billy's mind searched for a way out of this situation alive. *How can I possibly win?* He had no weapons. Or maybe he did. His memories whizzed across his mind's eye. He thought about Malyssa's healing power. He wasn't sure it would work, but it was worth a try.

"Come!" The Beast grabbed Billy's hand dragging him away, but suddenly let go shrieking in agony.

It was working; Billy was able to secrete poison through his skin from his frog Manifestus, onto The Beast.

"I'll kill you!" He screamed at Billy, launching himself forward and scratching and viciously clawing at Billy's body with his sharp taloned feet.

"Billy! Billy!" The calls rang on the air.

"Ugh! Leadbetter's!" cursed The Beast, suddenly manifesting and disappearing in a flash of white light.

Billy's body seared with pain, his own venom had trickled into his open wounds. He collapsed to the ground and his world went black.

The light initially hurt his eyes as Billy opened them for the first time in three days.

"He's waking up!" excited murmurs echoed around the dormitory. *No, it couldn't be the dormitory; Malyssa was there!* He looked closer at his surroundings: blue sleeping bag, blue curtains, bunch of boys all wearing blue...*it must be the Water House dormitory.*

"Where am I?" asked Billy groggily.

"In your bed in the dorm, Mate," said Jacob towering over him, that big white smile, brighter than the room.

"But...Malyssa's here," said Billy, utterly confused. Malyssa had hold of his hands.

"We thought we had better make an exception for Malyssa." A voice came from behind the heads of all the boys. The silver tipped spikes came into view. *Of course the kind voice belonged to Miss Leadbetter.* She was smiling.

"I'm pleased, but why?" asked Billy.

"She hasn't left your side for the three days you've been unconscious, tiring herself to the point of exhaustion, healing you."

Billy turned to smile at Malyssa. She looked over the top of her glasses. She had dark rings around her bloodshot eyes. She smiled, increasing the grip on his hands. "Thank you, Malyssa."

"We weren't sure she could do it," said Jacob.

"But clearly her gifts and talents exceed our expectations, as do yours," Miss Leadbetter turned to look at Jacob's leg, "and Jacob's." Jacob pulled at his collar and shifted his bandaged leg.

"You're OK?" asked Billy, remembering Jacob's injured leg.

"Yeah, Mr Leadbetter bandaged it up when he found

307

me, gave me some medicine, and then Malyssa has been healing me. She couldn't do it all in one go because she's been trying to rid you of poison."

"I'm sorry," said Billy feeling awkward.

"No, it's OK. I'd rather it was this way...I mean you dying would put a downer on this year, wouldn't it?" Jacob smirked at Billy.

"Ah, yes, well before we all get as emotional as Jacob," Miss Leadbetter winked at him, "Could I please have a moment with Billy alone?"

Without saying a word everyone left the room. Malyssa was so tired, she sort of shuffled across the wooden floor.

"Did he get away...I mean The Beast?"

"For now, yes," replied Miss Leadbetter. "Do you mind?" She gestured to the end of Billy's bed for her to sit down.

Billy shook his head.

"Thank you." She perched herself by his feet.

"Is he really my father?" Billy's voice trembled.

"Yes, of that I am certain," replied Miss Leadbetter placing a hand on Billy's foot.

"But how?"

"He and your mother were often together at The

Gifted Academy. He brought out a more confident side of your mother and she brought out a gentler side of him."

"Was he always this way?"

"No, no. He was always head strong, but as I said, your mother had a way with him that kept him grounded."

Billy could not imagine his mother bringing softer sides out of people, although her Christmas card to him may be a glimpse as to what she was like before the heartache.

"Why was she not with him?"

"They both finished here at The Gifted Academy at the end of year thirteen and the next thing we know is your mother had you and your father had reimagined himself as The Beast. You ended up living in the Humanum world as one of them."

Billy sighed deeply.

"What else is on your mind, Billy?"

"I-I manifested as a bird."

"Yes, Jacob said you had, but...we were not sure if he was delirious from blood loss."

"But, will I turn out the same as him?" He swallowed hard, scared of the answer.

"Only time will tell what you become," replied Miss Leadbetter, with a twinkle in her eye. "The Beast values the mind over the body and soul, but you don't have to. It is when all three work together harmoniously, that we can make good choices."

Knuckles rapped at the door to the dormitory, "I believe someone else wishes to have a private talk with you," she said to Billy. "Come in!" she called to the visitor. "I'll leave you to it." She smiled and walked away passing Mr Leadbetter as he entered the room avoiding eye contact with Billy. He crumpled onto the chair next to Billy; the one Malyssa had been sat in.

"I'm sorry, Billy," he said still unable to lift his head, "This was never supposed to happen."

Billy stayed silent.

"I hoped that I could change him, diminish the Manifestus temporarily and draw out his long squashed soul, b-but I failed him and I failed you, Billy. Please forgive me." His knee twitched nervously.

"I do, Sir," said Billy very matter-of-factly.

Mr Leadbetter looked up, Billy could see he hadn't shaved in a few days, or slept judging by the dark crescents under his eyes.

"Thank you, Dear Boy!" Mr Leadbetter stood up; a

new energy had surged through him, "Thank you." He made his way to the door, "I'm sure your friends would like to come back and see you before things return to normal for the remainder of the academic year." He lifted a hand to the door handle.

"Sir!" called Billy, "I'm sorry you couldn't save your brother."

Mr Leadbetter paused still facing the exit, "Me too, Billy, me too. I'll miss him, but he made his choices, as do we all, except some choices are better than others." Having said that, he pulled the door open and let it swing closed behind him.

Billy was made a fuss of for about a month before his near death experience became old news and everyone had more pressing needs to think about, like end of year exams, which Billy passed just fine.

Billy travelled in a rickety horse and cart back to the market place in the dishevelled clothes he had gone to The Gifted Academy in. His uniform was packed in his rucksack along with the crow study book from Miss Leadbetter and his frog in the glass bowl on his lap, croaking away, uncomfortable with the bumpy journey. His guitar case lent against his legs. The key in its pouch still hung round his neck.

Mr Shore would return him home from the market place.

Billy had lots of questions for his mother, but wasn't sure she'd answer them all, which was her choice. He didn't know what to expect when he got home.

He recalled the nightmare he had of his mother and sister; slaves to Manifestums and knew he would spend his life fighting for their freedom; dying for them if need be. That was his choice.

ABOUT THE AUTHOR

Hi there!

London based Children and Youth Worker, Linzi Golding, is an artist, a writer and author of several novels including THE ARTIST'S WARRIOR.

A professionally trained Primary School Teacher in the UK, Linzi has spent the last decade reading and writing fantasy fiction for children and youth. Children she has worked with often referred to her as 'Girl Peter Pan' for her ability to humorously act like a child – most of the time! Her latest work is a new expanded and illustrated edition of her first novel of the same title, The Artist's Warrior.

Linzi has been an avid reader and writer for as long as she can remember. As a child and teenager she won prizes for her stories and poetry and had a play script acted out by a local theatre when she was 13 years old!

Linzi was diagnosed with Autism at age 31 years and even though food is one of her favourite things in life, her obsession with reading and writing can often cause her to accidentally skip meals losing track of time and reality.

Get ready for the rest of the series following William 'Billy' Wortol!

For more information visit:

www.linzigolding.com

Follow Linzi Golding on Facebook

and Instagram

Look out for the next in the series...

The second in the series of seven books following William 'Billy' Wortol at The Gifted Academy.

COMING SOON...

Norman Lucky loves Christmas. And Father Christmas, the most infamous man in the world, is inviting six lucky people to his workshop at the North Pole. It's a once in a lifetime opportunity! Delicious treats, sleigh rides, (w)rapping elves and of course presents galore to be seen – Norman only needs to find one special letter with an invite included and this magical Christmas present could be his.

All books also available in dyslexia-friendly versions!

Printed in Great Britain
by Amazon